Hell Swamp

Susan Whitfield

L & L Dreamspell

Spring, Texas

ISBN: 978-1-60318-094-8

Library of Congress Control Number: 2008939285

Visit us on the web at www.lldreamspell.com

Published by L & L Dreamspell
Printed in the United States of America

Acknowledgements

Special thanks to my son, Graham, for proofing the work and offering scene suggestions from an avid hunter's perspective.

Thank you, Warren Cuddington, for the eagle eye help with sequence and to Robin Smith for editing suggestions.

Don Barnhill, I have a great appreciation for the history lesson about Black River and the real Hell Swamp, as well as for the awesome poem at the beginning of the novel.

Special thanks to Lisa Rene' Smith and the rest of the Dream Team for believing that I have something worthwhile to offer readers.

Words cannot express the gratitude I have for my family, friends, and fans. I love you all!

෨   ൙

Dedication:

For my sons,
Heath and Graham

HELL SWAMP

Out beyond the river wide
A swamp of ancient bogs
The place where only evil hides
Amid the rotted logs.
A wicked place, the devil's keep,
In darkness filled with fear
Lusting for a soul to reap
For death is always near.
Moss of green like putrid skin
You won't forget the smell
Of rotted leaf and hidden sin,
This swamp whose name is Hell.

Don Barnhill

One

"You'd better go easy on that breakfast buffet, Hunter. I need you in Pender County at Ivanhoe. I'm told it's a gruesome scene on Black River. Prepare yourself," said Kent Poletti, my supervisor. He'd spotted me slugging down my morning coffee and juice at the Grand Marquis Hotel breakfast buffet.

He tugged my arm, leading me away from the crowded 2008 North Carolina State Bureau of Investigation Conference meeting room. Poletti's voice sounded ragged, his face looked tired and stressed, and I couldn't help but notice he had started to gray since I last saw him. "Law enforcement has been told to rope off and wait for you and the coroner. And aren't you from that area anyway?"

"I once lived near that river, but sir…"

"No 'buts', Hunter. I need you. We're critically short-handed—half the force is passing some infernal virus back and forth to each other, and we're up to our collective asses in new cases."

"I lived in Atkinson just a few miles from the river as a child. But, sir, I'm supposed to be on leave right now." An uncharacteristic whine entered my voice.

"Forget leave. I'm assigning you to this case, Logan. I don't have a choice." He'd moved from my last name to first name. *I don't stand a damn chance.* His steel blue eyes held me like shackles while he spat out directions to the Corbett house, which sat just above the river in the tiny community of Ivanhoe. In the boonies, at least four hours away. I knew the house. I'd always liked that house, nestled in the bend of the river at Beatty's Bridge.

And forget leave?

This didn't sound like a case that could be solved in a hurry. I'd arranged to take a few days off so I could go home to Genesis Beach and make plans for my wedding. I'd come to Charlotte today, begrudgingly, and my vacation evaporated after one fricking day off! I hadn't even chosen my wedding gown.

Chase Railey, the love of my life, still worked in Asheville winding up a case before he came on board with the SBI. We'd planned to marry within the next six months, and hoped we could work on cases together as we had when we first met, thrown together by a serial killer in the Blue Ridge Mountains.

But now the wedding plans would have to wait. I mumbled obscenities, put the glass of juice on the table, and poured my coffee into a large Styrofoam cup that I could take with me.

Two

Black River has long been considered one of the cleanest rivers in North Carolina. I inhaled the scent of it, the Spanish moss, and the mustiness they created together. It had been several years since I'd traveled roads winding along beside and over it. My family lived near this river, and I swam in its cool refreshing waters every chance I got. Even though the water looked black, it remained relatively clear, stained by tree leaves, causing it to take on a dark coffee color from a distance. After we moved away, I relished the times we came back to visit old friends and swim in the river.

I drove my own Hummer rather than a state-issued sedan because I loved its power, and it kept the bureau from looming over my shoulder. Not that I planned to do anything illegal. I just liked my space, and I felt safe in my personal tank. I smiled as I raced by miles of white sand and pine trees strung with smothering vines of honeysuckle and kudzu. The narrow roads closest to the river wound their way through tired cotton patches, spent blueberry fields, and rows of exhausted day lilies, once vibrant yellow, orange, lavender, and blood red. I rolled down the windows, but the minute I realized my antihistamine provided no relief, they went right back up.

This time of year plants and weeds shit more pollen than I could endure. I coughed, sneezed, and hocked my way to a stop sign in the middle of nowhere. I opened the Hummer door and spit an unladylike wad of mucus out onto the pavement.

I straightened up and gasped. I'd driven over Beatty's Bridge numerous times over the years, but the old Greek Revival house always stopped me in my tracks. The closest thing around to a mansion, it sat in the curve just above the riverbank. Known by some as Black River Plantation, the locals called it The Corbett House. Still others called it "Rambling Rose", the set for a movie by the same name, starring Robert Duvall and Laura Dern back in the early nineties. A wealthy family built it, and I remembered one of my daddy's sisters-in-law living in it at one time, but I no idea who owned it now. Most locals, I suspected, didn't want to maintain it. Ancient oaks framed the front of the old apricot two-story house, each one dripping with Spanish moss. Now they seemed to loom ominously, perhaps because of the yellow crime tape stretched around them. Strobe lights from law-enforcement cruisers filled the yard with frantic flashes of blue and white light. Hoping the crime scene hadn't been compromised by all the activity, I turned my copper Hummer into the drive close enough to see cypress trees wading in the river that ambled by all the chaos.

I pulled up to the tape and flipped my sun visor down so the deputy could see my SBI identification. The young Pender County deputy tipped his hat, and once I'd parked, I followed him around to the front porch where a pudgy balding man in his mid-sixties stood, wiping his brow with a tan shirt sleeve bearing the Pender County Sheriff insignia. The little tuft of fuzz on the top of his head glistened with humidity.

"Ogden Gunn, Agent Hunter. I've had a hard time keeping down the dadgum spectators. Glad you could finally make it," he said. I didn't give the smart ass any response to his emphasis on "finally". He didn't smile. His face held wrinkles of a ghastly story. He walked me in the front door and announced my presence:

"The SBI's here. Now get your asses out of the way!"

The crowd parted to let us through—thirty or forty deputies from surrounding counties, according to their nametags, along with plenty of curiosity-seekers. Hot blood moved swiftly to my head in anger.

Why were all these people allowed in here?

Once the crowd slid out of the way I could see why they all gawked. The naked body of a tiny woman, gutted from chin to anus like a deer, hung from the chandelier. I gulped. My eyes fixated in disbelief, but I forced them up: the top of a skinning gambrel was hooked to a fancy light fixture by a three-pronged iron grapple. The victim's heel tendons had been cut so the gambrel, hoisted by a rope and pulley, could go through. Everywhere my eyes focused, they found horror. They settled on her head, matted with blood, near the floor. I couldn't have recognized her even if I'd known her. Bloody entrails oozed in all directions over the floor. A shredded pile of fabric resembled clothing.

Had she been alive when her heels were slit? When the knife ripped her open?

I froze in front of what appeared to be her liver. I grabbed the sheriff's arm for physical support and to get his attention.

"Get these people outta here!" I took a staccato breath. "Where's the medical examiner?"

"All we've got is the county coroner, Agent Hunter. There's no ME in this county." Gunn pointed to the colorless old gentleman sitting on the bottom stair, drinking what appeared to be bourbon straight from a glass decanter. The room cleared with grunts, grumbles, and ugly stares as I approached the coroner.

"Lemmie Sawyer." His weak voice eked from the bottle's lip. "I've been going to death scenes for fifty years. Wrecks. Murders. Suicides. I've never seen anything to compare with this." He shook his head.

"Sir, I don't suppose you brought that decanter from home?"

He turned from pale green to red.

"Oh. I didn't think. I'm sorry, Investigator. I just grabbed it off the bar yonder."

I turned to look at a mahogany bar filled with glass decanters of dark liquids and turned back to Gunn.

"Listen, Sheriff, we've got a hell of a mess here. All these people have trampled the crime scene and this…this man over here took a decanter of whiskey from the bar! Why didn't you secure this scene?" I felt like slapping him half to death.

"Look, Agent Hunter, I'm upset too, but blasting me won't help none. Some of these folks got here way before I did. It took me a good thirty minutes of hard driving to get here after the dispatch. The word got out on a scanner. Everybody around here has one."

Great. That's just freaking great. I could feel my teeth clenching with tension.

I told him to please keep anything else from being touched. I could tell he felt embarrassed, as well he should be. I wondered how much of the crime scene had been compromised.

Probably all of it from the look of things.

The front door, the foyer, and the staircase, for certain. Bloody shoeprints covered the wood floor in every possible direction. This constituted an investigator's worst nightmare, and I owned it.

My hand trembled as I eased the SavvyCam from my pocket to take pictures of the atrocity from every angle. With this little workhorse I could record my findings as well as photograph every piece of latent evidence found. Even though I felt it disrespectful to the dead, I couldn't leave all this to recollection, so I steadied myself and started clicking.

I moved around the room, taking one shot after another, recording my findings and thoughts in a whisper and shaking my head in disbelief. Blood pooled and dripped everywhere, especially around the victim, a woman, presumed to be Clara Banoak. Her innards spilled in spattered bloody batches all over the parquet floor. The formerly white walls now looked like the masterpiece of some perverted abstract painter. The red spatters reached to the second floor walls, and many stair steps held big red globs of stain.

A brocade loveseat sat under the stair alcove, with plenty of blood soaked into its fabric. A small cream table lamp and shade atop an antique desk were also blotched with stain. With a gloved hand, I moved the loveseat enough to see something metal. I eased around and picked up bent wire-framed glasses.

"Did Clara Banoak wear glasses?"

"Yeah." I looked up. Lemmie Sawyer approached. "What you got?"

I showed him the glasses. "Yep, they look like hers. She couldn't see a damn thing without them."

I labeled and bagged them, handing them to Gunn so I could get back to my task.

I directed my next question to the coroner. "Mr. Sawyer, do you think she was alive when this started?"

"I'll get back to you on that. Lord knows I hope she was already dead," the coroner said.

"Look," I said, sticking out a hand to him, "I apologize if I acted rude. It's just that this investigation is going to be *my* nightmare."

"It's me who should apologize. By being too shocked to think straight, I hope I didn't contribute to the mess."

Unsure of exactly what to say, I didn't respond.

"I need the sheriff. Where did Gunn go?"

"Over here." Gunn stuck his head around a doorframe and sauntered over to me.

"Sheriff, there should be prints on the gambrel and maybe we can get something—maybe some DNA off the rope, I don't know. Have your detective check all sales of rope and gambrels to anyone in this area. The gambrel most likely came from a catalog."

"Yes, ma'am, and every deer hunter's got at least one."

"Then see who's missing one."

"This is gone take manpower, Agent Hunter. I've only got two deputies on this side of the county."

Why do I always end up with the rural crimes?

I already knew the answer to that one. I grew up not too far from here, a country girl. I'd never lived in a city. I knew what to look for, what seemed out of place in a country setting. A city agent might not single out those clues as quickly, and I would probably miss some key evidence if assigned to a big-city case by myself.

I glanced at Gunn. "I'll call for another agent." I wanted Chase.

As the sheriff wandered off, I called Kent Poletti at SBI Headquarters and filled him in on the situation.

"Logan, I can't help you. I realize that's a tough situation down there. But nothing's changed up here in the past few hours. We're still short-handed because of that damn virus, and I'm working eighteen-hour shifts myself. In fact, Railey is one of the few agents still standing."

"Good. Send him down here," I almost demanded with glee.

"No can do. He's on another case and I can't afford to move him right now. Logan, you're pretty much on your own. I'm sorry. Just put on your big-girl panties and do whatever it takes to get the monster. I do have Wiley Savage on the way to do some lab work, but you can only have him today."

He hung up before I could respond. I wouldn't allow most men to get away with that panty remark. In his case, however, I understood what he meant and knew he intended no sexual connotation.

I needed to solve this case on my own with what little local law-enforcement I had at my disposal. Law-enforcement with more experience supervising ball games than investigating murders. They were fortunate to serve in a low-crime area. I needed expert help, but my options were limited.

Wanting to at least hear Chase's voice, I dialed his cell and left a message on his voice mail before taking a deep breath and going back inside to deal with the horror. I walked through the front door and into the first adjoining room, which apparently functioned as a den. With a gloved hand, I reached for a picture of the victim in happier times. Not a handsome woman even then, Clara Banoak's mousy straight brown hair fell over protruding ears where her dark wire-framed glasses hooked. The puke-green sweater she wore didn't help matters.

Yep. Mousy covered it. But she looked harmless. Why would anyone strike out at her in such a horribly sadistic way?

I clicked my cam then looked at Lemmie Sawyer.

"Can you estimate the time of death?"

"It's gone be hard to determine since she's been gutted and hung like that. That'd cool the body in a hurry. I'd guess sometime in the early evening since it looks like she had some things out to cook but never cooked them."

"Murder weapon? Motive?" I quizzed Sawyer as he dragged himself up from a crouched position.

"Right off-hand, I'd say a dressing knife, the kind hunters skin a deer with." He waited for my reaction.

"A little bizarre, don't you think?"

"Agent Hunter, Clara Banoak hated hunters around here and they hated her. Everybody knows that. Not just deer hunters either. All hunters."

Sheriff Gunn, now by my side, looked anxious. "Can we cut her down and let Lemmie take her in? She's been hanging there since last night sometime." I nodded and walked into the kitchen. I didn't want to see Clara Banoak's remains hit the floor.

The kitchen in the old house appeared to have been recently updated. The warm olive walls complimented the white cabinets. A crystal vase filled with fresh flowers from somewhere sat on the curved dark granite island. Neat. Clean. Not much to indicate what time she died.

Lemmie correctly analyzed the situation. A cookbook stood open on a stand and the stainless steel range held a spaghetti pot and a red teakettle. The cabinet light over the cookbook glared down on a recipe. Completely thawed bags of vegetables—broccoli and squash—leaked cloudy fluid into the stainless steel sink. Several yellow plates and folded linen napkins rested on the counter.

Had she invited her killer to eat with her?

Lemmie would try to determine that.

I went from the front door to the other exterior doors, including the one that led out onto a screened porch and faced the highway. No sign of forcible entry.

Did Clara Banoak know her murderer? Had she willingly let him—or them—in? Could one person manage all this alone? And why split her open?

Tiny hairs rose on my arm as a chill skittered down it. I saw something across the porch near the screen, and walked over and picked up a cigarette butt, bagged, and labeled it.

Did Clara Banoak smoke? Or had her killer enjoyed a satisfying after-murder smoke before he left?

"Agent Hunter?"

A tall, good-looking man about my age, walked across the yard toward the porch at a slow pace.

"Yes?"

"Wiley Savage, ma'am. I'm from the SBI lab."

"Wow! You must have been on the road before I called Poletti. He said to expect you."

"Yes, he knew you needed some help, and I came from Salemburg, not Raleigh, so it didn't take too long."

"Come on in, Savage, but you might want to take a deep breath first."

We walked through the kitchen without a word, and I showed him into the front foyer where the body still hung.

"Jesus Christ!" Wiley looked away and then slowly turned his eyes up and followed the gambrel down to the floor. "I don't know how Poletti thinks you can do this without some assist."

"According to him, most of the agents have come down with some illness that isn't responding to antibiotics. I have no choice."

"Yes, he's got me strung out from here to New Bern and back to Winston-Salem, and needs everything I can find yesterday."

We watched as Gunn and his men eased Clara Banoak's remains to the body bag on the floor. Savage took out a penlight and examined the corpse, finding and extracting a few strands of hair. I handed him a plastic bag to drop each one in, and let him label them. Once he inspected the body to his satisfaction, we motioned to the other men to bag it. Lemmie zipped it up. We followed them out the door and to a waiting EMS truck that would transport the remains to the coroner's office in Burgaw. Only then did we speak again.

"I, um." The lab technician shook his head slowly. "That's atrocious." Savage, noticeably weak in the knees, eased around the room. He cleared his throat but managed to keep down any food he'd eaten in the past few hours and stay on his feet. "I'll, uh, bag up the bloody entrails and use a vacutainer to gather as much blood as possible. The coroner has his work cut out for him." He sighed. "No pun intended."

I nodded.

We went back inside, and I proceeded around the room and toward the staircase. "Have fun, Savage. I'll call you if I find anything upstairs that needs your attention." As I looked at the first stair, I spotted a small gold hoop earring. I picked it up and walked outside with it in my gloved hand.

"Check her ear and see if she's missing an earring." Lemmie walked over to the bag and unzipped it. He and Gunn both nodded.

"Yep, the left one's missing."

"A gold hoop?"

"It's gold," said the coroner. "Ogden, is that a hoop?"

"Damn if I know. I guess."

Geez Loueez!

I walked over to have a look for myself. "Gentlemen, that is a gold hoop. That's your lesson in jewelry for today."

They sauntered off, rolling their eyes but not saying a word to me. I bagged and labeled the earring. Once Savage and I both approved, Lemmie Sawyer left the yard with the body.

Most local law enforcement cleared out to go spread the gruesome story to anybody who would listen. Sheriff Gunn, Wiley

Savage, and I remained. I pulled on paper slippers and climbed the stairs, careful to skip those with large amounts of blood drying into the carpet fibers. At the top I took a left and opened a bedroom door. A picture of a woman resembling Clara Banoak sat on the bureau.

So she had a daughter.

"That's me." The voice came from behind me, giving me a start. I turned to face her. She had the same mousy brown hair, but longer and more becoming, and the same mouth as the victim. But her nose reminded me of the curve in a coat hanger, a little too long and sharp to be attractive. She twisted her leopard print scarf over her dung-brown sweater. If she wore make-up, it didn't show. She hadn't used a teeth-whitening strip in a long time, either.

"Nita Quicki. Daughter." Her voice trembled.

"Logan Hunter, SBI. I'm sorry about your mother, Ms. Quicki." She nodded and left the room.

I followed.

"Ms. Quicki, do you live here?"

"No, in Wilmington."

"How long have you been here at the crime scene?"

"Since I found Mama."

"Sheriff Gunn didn't tell me you were here." I reached for my cam and mashed the *Record* button. "I need to ask you some questions."

She waved me off. "I've already told Sheriff Gunn that I walked in the back door and called out to her. She planned to cook some pasta and make a salad for my birthday."

"Today is your birthday?"

"Yesterday, actually. She wanted to cook for me last night, but I called her at the last minute to tell her I sold a house and just couldn't get up here." She took out a cigarette, but never placed it between her lips. "If I had been here, this wouldn't have happened."

"Or you would have been a victim too." She looked into my

eyes and then dropped her head. "I'm sorry. I know this has to be terribly difficult. Was anyone else coming for dinner?"

"She invited Marvin, my ex, but I never told him. I thought it would be better if it were just the two of us. Just Mama and me." The woman touched a couple of items on the hall table. I cringed.

"Look, you shouldn't be here. I'll walk you out. I can ask you more later." She glared at me. "I mean, this house is now a crime scene. Nothing, and I do mean nothing, should be touched."

"I guess you didn't see the throng downstairs?" Her unpleasant tone didn't sit well with me.

"Yes, but we ushered them out. You could be disturbing evidence up here, Ms. Quicki. Not intentionally, of course. At this point we have no idea what happened. Everything has to be investigated, every room, every wall, every piece of paper, the whole ball of wax."

Her facial expression changed to one of sadness and the tears started to trickle.

"Look, Ms. Quicki, I'm truly sorry, but…"

She threw out a hand. "I understand. Really." We walked to the staircase and maneuvered around the bloodstains, across the gory foyer and into the front yard.

"I'll need to ask hard questions, but we can do it later. Does the sheriff have your address?"

"Yes, but I'll be back tomorrow, I promise you. I already told the sheriff I couldn't imagine who'd do such an awful thing." She sat on a cement bench between the house and the river, placed the well-rubbed cigarette into a long holder she had taken from her pocket, and lit it, blowing smoke right at me, the same brand as the butt I'd bagged on the screened porch.

I coughed and waved my arm to indicate my displeasure. "Did your mother live here alone?"

"Yes." She paid no attention to my annoyance, puffing toward me again.

"It's kind of isolated, don't you think?"

"She loved it. Wouldn't you?" We both remained quiet long enough to hear the soft lull of the river current. "She and my daddy moved here years ago so he could fish and paint and she could write poetry. All those pictures around the house are Daddy's. He died about five years ago. He's buried near the river. Mother wouldn't leave. And she never did write any decent poetry."

"Did she have any enemies you're aware of?"

A curt laugh. "Yes, indeed, she did. I wouldn't know where to begin. You see, my mother was an animal-rights activist, which in and of itself isn't a bad thing, but she took it to the extreme. This is hunting country, Agent Hunter. She pissed off lots of hunters. It was a constant thing, year in and year out. I tried to get her to move to Wilmington—as much for the hunters as for her—but she refused and insisted they weren't going to run her off her land."

"Any specific names?"

"She's had run-ins with every hunter in this county and plenty from other places."

"Did they trespass on the property to hunt?"

"No, as far as I know none of them ever did anything to her. They were *her* victims, Agent Hunter. She took several newspapers, *The Wilmington Morning Star, The Pender Chronicle* and *The Post, The Sampson Independent,* and even *The Bladen Times.* If a hunter had his picture in any paper with a trophy deer, bear, or whatever, she'd cut out the picture, track down an address, and mail the picture with a few choice comments, like 'Murderer' or 'You ought to be shot', or something along those lines."

"That's bold."

"No fear. That was my mother. She had no fear at all. And there was no arguing with her either. You might as well forget it. She got worse after Daddy died. She became totally unreasonable with hunters wanting to kill any animal. But not just hunters. She'd go after anyone who mistreated a pet or a farm animal too." Nita Quicki rose.

"Did you say you live in Wilmington?"

"Yes. My ex, Marvin, and I own Quicki Realty together."

"So your name is Nita Banoak Quicki, for the record."

"Well," she managed a broad smile, "I've been married five times. How technical do you want to get?"

"Any hunters in the bunch?"

"Uh, yeah, but what are you implying?"

"I have to check out all family members as well as anyone else of interest." She reluctantly gave me the names of each of her exes.

"You've got quite a job ahead of you then, Agent Hunter. Here's my card. Call me if you find the bastard. I'd personally like to castrate him."

She walked to a red convertible; Gunn strolled over and gave her a hug. His balding head sweated profusely, I supposed from the grisly scene coupled with the smothering humidity, common in eastern North Carolina even into late fall. We watched Nita Quicki drive away before we spoke.

"Sheriff, we need to find out who's killed a deer and had a picture in the newspaper recently."

He nodded. "Deer season just started. That shouldn't be too hard to find out. You thinking Clara pissed off a hunter right to start with?"

"It's a possibility. Look, I'll get my evidence kit and gather these clothes, but they have to air dry. Maybe we'll get lucky and find some of the killer's DNA on them," I said.

"We'll get the gambrel and rope down and bagged." He looked me in the eye. "You think we can pick up prints on them?"

"It's worth a try. That is, if he didn't wear gloves. I'd assume at the moment he—or they—did, since this operation had to be premeditated."

Sheriff Gunn wrote in a journal. "I've logged who's been in and out and what time Lemmie left with the body." He handed me the journal. "Actually, Agent Hunter, to be honest, I got all the names I could remember, but there were so many people in there. We just couldn't stop them once the word got out." He punched numbers into his cell phone.

"I know. But we can't let the murderer get away because of a compromised crime scene. We have to find the trace evidence and solve this case. Nobody should get away with something this heinous. I've got a black light. I want to check tracks inside and outside the house. Maybe we can figure out how many attackers there were and if they came in from front and back."

"You mean like an ambush?"

"Anything is possible," I responded.

I hushed as the sheriff spoke to someone on his phone.

"Yeah. Okay. Thanks, Dora." Gunn closed his phone. "It seems the paper hasn't run any deer pictures yet this season. It's early. She said they'd probably have some in the next week or so."

"So if this is the revenge of a hunter, it's carried over from a previous year."

"You have to remember there's all kinds of hunting seasons, not just deer. And we're not even sure it was a hunter."

"You're right, of course. Somebody could have set it up to look like a hunter did it, but that's an awful lot of trouble to go to. I mean, with the gutting and stringing her up like that."

I retrieved my black light from the Hummer and went over the house carefully, checking to see if the killer attempted to cover up blood in other areas of the house. Pristine walls and floors, everywhere except in the large foyer and staircase, showed Clara Banoak's attention to detail and cleanliness. The initial attack, I surmised, took place in the entrance foyer. Then the victim was hoisted. The hemorrhaged organs would have dripped and spattered once the jugular ejected the bulk of the blood.

Even after I'd been out in the fresh air for a while I could still smell Clara Banoak's blood—never an odor I could get accustomed to. After I finished my work at the crime scene, I stopped at Yonder Store, a little gas station in the fork of a road, hoping they had some peppermints to get the smell out of my sinuses. Relieved that the little store *Open* sign still blinked, I walked around the shelves and approached the woman behind the counter who read from a magazine and paid no attention to me.

"Ma'am?"

"Yes?"

"Do you have any peppermint candy?"

"What candy we got is so old I'd be afraid for you to eat it."

"Okay. How about salsa?"

She laughed and shook her head. "What are you trying to do? I know you're the SBI agent. I already heard about you, and you look like one."

"Yes, ma'am. Well, there are several remedies we use to get the smell of fresh blood out of our sinuses. I'm trying to avoid the other option."

"Which is?"

"Horseradish."

"Oh, we keep some of that on hand."

Why does that not surprise me?

Three

The hand wrapped around my throat, its long nails cutting my skin. I screamed. I could hear myself screaming. I snatched myself from the fingers' grip and fell. I fell a long way, and lay still, feeling the pain in my back. Dirt hit my face.

I'm being buried alive!

I scrambled sideways when I realized nothing held me in place. When I hit the table, I woke up, sprawled on the floor, my aloe plant from the bedside table and all its dirt on top of me. My night terrors had returned, more frightening than ever. I sat up on the floor and spit out dirt, flipping the plant onto the floor. I had peed in my pants.

2:47 a.m., and I was wide-awake, clogged up in spite of a couple of doses of straight horseradish, and totally unnerved. The previous day's discovery left me troubled. It went with the territory, but the cases I got just seemed to get progressively more violent. I recalled the bloody liver on the floor, one of many internal organs found around Clara Banoak's foyer. I shivered and groaned at the memory.

I couldn't figure out why the recurring night terrors that haunted me throughout the Teater murder case, my first investigation, returned. I took medication for a year back then, and never got the prescription renewed. They seemed to be gone once I'd confronted the man who'd molested small children in our church. While I'd never been certain I was one of his victims, I knew that he had, at least, attempted to molest me.

Now this new case brought my demons back to the surface, and I didn't need this kind of distraction and energy-robber.

I trudged off to my kitchen and made some chai tea to chase down two antihistamine tablets, hoping they would unclog my nasal congestion without making me lethargic. I'd driven the two hours home from the crime scene since I had no place to stay up there. I'd thought I'd rest better in my own condominum at Genesis Beach. So much for that idea. I gulped hot tea and stared out at the sound as a yacht sailed toward the Intra-Coastal Waterway.

I intended to strike out again early, to walk the Banoak property, and go over the house with less interference from other folks. I expected the sheriff would be nearby though. Thankful that Poletti assigned Chase to help me, it would still be several more days before he could get here and be valuable. Chase, a veritable bloodhound once he got on the right track, didn't leave the trail until he had his man. We made an awesome team. I smiled, looking forward to reuniting with him. Touching him, kissing him, holding him—all the breathtaking feelings I'd thought a year ago I could never have for any man.

I again thought of my night terrors and how I'd survived the realization I might have been molested as a child. By a preacher of all people. Rick Teater's father. The nightmares, or night terrors, as the doctor called them, had tormented me. Medicine and an empathetic shrink helped me through the hard times, along with my pal, Pepper, who gave me the Hummer as a gift, in what I'd considered a fit of insanity at the time. She'd insisted she could afford it, having been named the lone beneficiary of Rick Teater's multi-million dollar estate.

My ownership of the Hummer and my friendship with Pepper were now two years old. I needed to call her; it had been a while since we'd spoken. I wouldn't bring up the return of the terrors. It would be more fun to talk about the wedding. I expected her to be my only attendant, and she insisted on catering the entire event through her restaurant.

Ogden Gunn handed me a cold drink as we walked out the back door and headed toward the river.

"Any ideas, Sheriff?"

"We didn't find any fresh tracks in the driveway, possibly because of the storm last night. That dadgum rain robbed us of any evidence that might have been out there. Removed any possible vehicle tracks." He looked toward the river. "There's no way to know for sure, but the killer could have come by boat. Let's take a look around." We headed over the slight embankment and scoured the edges of the river near a dilapidated boat dock. I picked up a scrap of black cloth, but we found nothing more. The fabric, a cotton material, appeared to have been ripped from a larger piece of fabric. I trained my eyes on the ground and culled anything that could tear clothing. I tucked the cloth into a zip-lock bag and labeled it in case, at some point, it became evidence.

"Did Clara Banoak own a boat?"

"Not for years, at least not one decent enough to get on the water with. Eli used to fish some, but I'm not aware she ever took the boat out after he died. Of course, I don't live here, so's I don't know for sure."

"Do many people use the river to travel?"

"No, not much anymore. Mostly campers and fishermen. The hurricanes of the past ten years have toppled quite a few trees in that river, and it can be treacherous at night, even with a spotlight. But if someone wanted to sneak up, it's mighty dark and not likely there'd be any witnesses either. I'll get some men to go over this area thoroughly." I nodded agreement. "You may want to check out the put-ins over yonder yourself." He pointed to the landings on either side of the bridge some two hundred yards away.

"There's easy access from both sides."

"So the killer could have actually driven here, backed in, taken his own boat across, killed Banoak, gone back across and loaded his boat and left."

"Yep, it's possible. It's too dark to see anything at night though, unless the moon is full term. Eli never wanted the yard lights that come on by themselves at dusk. Too citified for him, I reckon. Most folks on the river use spotlights or lanterns to get around."

The sheriff touched my arm and cleared his throat. "Agent Hunter, I want to apologize if I got short with you yesterday. It's just that I've never seen such a brutal murder. People were showing up and God knows what they touched or stepped in before we could contain things. I reckon it just got to me. I didn't mean to be rude. I'm glad the SBI is involved. I don't have the knowledge and skill to handle this alone. This county has mighty few officers and they don't have to deal with much violence, I'm glad to say. Nothing gory like this mess. I'll help you any way I can. I'm at your disposal."

"Thank you, and no apologies are necessary. Let's just get them and fast."

"Them?"

"That's my theory, at least for the time being. It seems too difficult to hang her up without some help. There's no blood smeared on the staircase. It looks like they took her up the stairs, lifted her over, and just dropped her. Maybe after her heels were split and she was put on the gambrel. One person would have had to drag her up the staircase and drop her over the rail. I don't see one person doing all that and attaching the grapple to the chandelier. No, it seems to me there has to be more than one killer."

The sheriff scratched his head. "That's a good observation, I reckon. That's why we need you so much. It never occurred to me there might be more than one killer. I find that even more unsettling." He faced me. "I'm sure you've heard Clara wasn't exactly Miss Congeniality. She had a way of minding everybody else's business, and that riled folks."

"Especially hunters, I understand."

"Well, yeah, but you can hardly blame 'em for hating her. She stayed after 'em like a horsefly on dog shit. I reckon Nita told you about Clara's obsession with AFTA, The Association for Fair Treatment of Animals. Not that there's anything wrong with that, but Clara went too far. She thought everybody ought to be vegetarian like her. She said all animals ought to be left alone to wander wherever they wanted to. Can you imagine having to stop your Hummer every time a cow wanted to cross the road?

"Clara believed animals shouldn't be eaten for any reason. Not deer, and not even cows. She made a scene at church if she heard somebody say they were having roast for supper. She pissed off just about everybody."

The sheriff looked at the ground and kicked some dirt before clearing his throat again. "I might as well go ahead and tell you I took her out a couple of times, years ago, after Eli died, but I couldn't take her any place that she didn't end up causing a scene. She was intelligent, I guess, and could make good conversation, but it always got back to the same topic. It was too dadgum embarrassing to be seen with her. I suspect more than one person wanted her dead."

"Thanks for letting me know that, Sheriff. I need all the knowledge you can share on Clara." I handed him a piece of paper. "These are all Nita's ex-husbands. And besides them, there's a sizable list of other possible suspects. This investigation is going to take a while."

He studied the list and pointed to one of the names. "But you can take Chub Dowdy off."

"Why is that?"

"He's dead. Ole Chub," he said, shaking his head before looking at me. "Nita married Acme and stayed married to him a good while. When that marriage went south, she took off and married Sly Foxx, a much younger, good-looking man. It shocked the whole blasted county to hear about that one. They had it annulled fast. Sly says they were both drunk. In no time Nita did a three-sixty and married Chub, an old, fat, bald man. He had some money, and I really think she went after that, and poor ole

Chub just had the hots for her."

"How did he die?"

"Some people think Nita wanted too much from him physically, if you know what I mean. He had a massive heart attack, naked, right in his bed, and never regained consciousness. He left her plenty of money though, but it didn't last long."

"So she buried him and ran through the money?"

"No, she was fairly frugal as far as I know. Did a little investing, I heard. But she was reckless. Nita doesn't like being alone. She soon hooked up with Braxton Huff, another name on your list, and a real piece of work. Nobody around knew him, just a drifter who showed up here. A sweet-talking son of a gun. Swept her right off her feet. They flew somewheres and got hitched. Nita made the mistake of opening a joint bank account after that."

"Uh-oh."

"Yes, ma'am. He cleaned her out and disappeared. He's probably in the Caribbean right now, sipping on a cold beverage with a sweet young thing."

"You don't think Braxton Huff came back and knocked off Clara?"

"Not likely. He wasn't around her enough to have any feelings about her one way or the other. He's not your man."

"Wow, what a life Nita has, huh?" He nodded. "Oh, Sheriff, I may need some office space to sort through all this and to do some interrogating. I can't guarantee you I'd ever get there, but sometimes it helps to have a space to spread things out and maybe do some serious intimidating." I put a dark line through Chub Dowdy's name and a question mark beside Huff's.

"I've got a small office open. I'll get it cleaned up, and you can use it any time you want to."

"Thanks. I've already got such a list of people to question I think we'd better Mirandize them all, just in case."

"Read 'em all their rights? They'll think they're being arrested. That might not go down too easy, Agent Hunter."

"We'll be diplomatic. Just a precautionary measure." I could tell the sheriff didn't like my idea. "Marandizing any possible suspects might save our butts in the end. I'd rather err on the side of caution."

"Well, it's your call, of course. Oh, by the way, Nita's alibi checks out. She sold a house on the night her mother died. A couple flew in late at night from California, and she showed me the forms where they dated and even put the time. It was 1:45 in the morning and then she checked them into a hotel."

How convenient.

"Thanks for taking the initiative on that."

"I knew she'd be considered a prime suspect since she stands to inherit everything Eli and Clara accumulated."

"Yep, family members are almost always on the list until they prove their whereabouts."

I slapped my arm. "Ow! Something just bit me."

"That would be the shit flies."

"Shit flies?"

"Yeah, they bite the shit outta 'ya." He grinned as I scratched and looked around for more possible attackers. "We also have No-see-ems. They're so tiny you can't even find 'em to kill. They go right through the dadgum window screens. Some people call 'em Teeth."

Great. I'll be eaten alive. My next stop would be a Deep Woods Off counter if I could find one within thirty miles.

We followed a grassy path edged with plush hostas and goldenrods over an old cobblestone creek bridge, and around the edge of a bed of purple asters. A neglected tombstone caught my eye: *Joseph Elijah Banoak. Rest in Peace.* Weeds hid the dates. I walked over and pulled them up. I figured Clara would soon be in the plot beside him.

Corpses of corn stood in the field I trudged through. In the distant woods, leaves on deciduous trees were turning from green to orange, from orange to yellow and from yellow to dead brown.

Fall had arrived.

The buck-toothed Latino girl I'd talked to at the farmhouse followed me from a distance. She'd told me in broken English that the man I wanted to talk with was in the field with the workers, gathering the dried corn for late market. I tried to walk in the bumpy rows between the scraggly stalks, but found it difficult to stay the course.

"Ahh…choo!" My clogged head didn't make walking through a dusty cornfield pleasant.

"Bless you," the girl said. I estimated her age around ten or eleven. I looked back to thank her, but she had disappeared.

I stepped into the open as a farmhand pointed at me from a distance and yelled something in Spanish while others stopped working and stared at me. A man wearing a camo cap turned in my direction and waited for me to come to him. I felt as though one hundred eyes stared at me, more than likely wondering why a strange woman appeared from the cornfield.

"Agent Hunter. SBI," I stated, showing my badge and dusting off my black pants.

"Hawk Daw."

Daw, the first name on my list who wasn't one of Nita's exes, stood eye-to-eye with me. He had chubby cheeks even though he wasn't chubby, and a thick reddish mustache, although his dark brown hair didn't match. He didn't smile or offer to shake my hand, so I got down to business.

"I'm investigating the murder of Clara Banoak. I need to ask you some questions. I can see you're busy now. When's a good time for you?"

"This evening, I reckon. But I'm gone get this corn to market first, before all the rain that's forecast sets in." He took off his cap and scratched his sweaty head. "Yeah, this evening. I ought to be back around nine o'clock. Just come to the house up there." He pointed.

"If you walk straight up the clearing, you'll find a dirt road. Those kids should have told you that." He smiled for the first time.

I thanked him and started walking toward the road.

He didn't have much to say, at least not yet. I'd be back at nine o'clock. I reached the Hummer where several children studied it like a science project. I answered a few questions about it and left them staring after me.

I headed for the next name on my list, Acme Beavers. I stopped at Yonder Store to ask directions, and walked in as a man with short frizzy hair approached. His freckled face reminded me of a navel; everything drew in to the ugly little opening called a mouth.

"Excuse me, sir, can you tell me where a Mr. Acme Beavers lives?" I showed him my badge and ID.

The navel puckered and spoke. "He works at the pulpwood plant at Riegelwood and never gets home until around six o'clock." The navel...uh, the man gave me directions to the Beavers residence and I jotted down a note to be there around six. I climbed back into the Hummer as a red Chevrolet Silverado pulled up and a man got out, tipping his purple East Carolina Pirate baseball cap to me.

I rolled down my window. "Excuse me, sir, you wouldn't be Edsel Foxx, would you?"

"How'd you know that? Do I know you?" Cute, with his head covered in wavy red hair and his freckled skin with a nose that reminded me of a ski jump. Mr. Foxx had a broad smile and eyes that resembled chocolate chips. He exuded charm. I had long ago learned to watch out for the charismatic ones because they usually hid something.

I stepped out of the Hummer. "I'm Logan Hunter, SBI agent, investigating Clara Banoak's murder." We shook hands. "I understand you married her daughter."

"I figured you'd come looking for me but not this quick. Nita called me."

This ex-husband looked younger than Nita by quite a few years.

"We weren't married long enough to say it counts. We had it

annulled three days later—a big drunken mistake."

Is he reading my mind?

"But you did know Clara Banoak?"

"Yes, ma'am. Everybody around here knows Clara."

"Did you like her?"

He showed me the palms of both hands. "Whoa now. Hold on. I'm not sure I like the way you're questioning me. She had plenty of enemies. Yes, she pitched a fit about Nita marrying me. Yes, she was right about that. She got no argument from me. I got out of it as fast as I could." He shuffled his feet and looked down the road. "Look, I'm on my way home. I work night shift. Give me a couple of hours to sleep and I'll be glad to talk to you. I'm a zombie right now. I live down this road," he said, pointing his freckled arm. "Cross the bridge and take a left on Hound Dog Road. You'll see lots of trees hanging with moss. My house sits back off the road. How about three o'clock this evening?"

I agreed, jotting down the directions.

A bright yellow short-bed truck pulled up as Mr. Foxx turned around. A diminutive man got out. "How ya doing, Sly?"

"Hey, Coon."

I craned my neck. "Coon? Would you, by chance, be Woody Forbesch?"

"Yes'm, but everybody calls me Coon 'cause I've killed more coons than anybody in this county." He threw out his hand as I introduced myself. Another person on my list of interesting people. I learned that he operated a store just down the road. I told him I would drop by.

I already had appointments at three, six, and nine, so I would have to work Coon in later. The other name on my list was Cyrano Blood, not one of Nita Quicki's exes. I hadn't met him, but I'd learned he lived on an isolated farm down the river at a place named Bear Creek Swamp, and he drove an unsightly yellow and gray pickup with the bed rusted out.

I needed to find a place to stay since I intended to stay until I had some answers, and I'd packed a duffel bag just in case this investigation took a great deal of time. I rode to Burgaw about fifteen miles away and found my only option there, The Azalea Motel, under major reconstruction. Atkinson and Ivanhoe, both closer to the crime scene, had no motel, no B&B, no lodging of any kind. The other choice: bedding down in the Hummer. I didn't want driving all the way back to Genesis Beach to be a daily necessity. Time and gas prices were top issues. I had no time to try to find an old friend to stay with. Besides, I didn't want to involve too many folks in this awful mess.

I picked up the prescription Dr. Rivenbark called in for my night terrors, promising him I would make an appointment if they persisted. I pulled into a drive-thru in the tiny town and picked up a fresh burger combo, swung around and screeched off, heading back to the crime scene.

I parked along the dark country road where I could keep the Banoak property in sight and ate the rest of my food. From my angle I saw where the backyard met the river and where the highway curved around the majority of the house. As it started to rain, I pulled a fleece blanket from the back and snuggled down to rest while I tried to subdue the burger burps. Having a few peaceful minutes with the quiet rain tapping on the Hummer's roof pleased me.

After a while my cell rang and brought me to attention. "Hunter."

Sheriff Gunn said, "Agent Hunter, we found a gut hook skinner after you left the scene. It could be the murder weapon."

"Where are you now?"

"I'm almost back to the office in Burgaw."

"Good. Bag it, and I'll get someone to pick it up from your office. I don't suppose it's rare?"

"No such luck, ma'am. Every hunter in North America has one of these babies."

That's what I was afraid he'd say.

I yawned and stretched out my long arms. Everything looked polished after the downpour. I got out and stretched my legs before heading for the property belonging to the next name on the list.

On the way, I saw a farmhouse and shed painted rusty red that sat in the middle of a field, shaded by a pecan grove. I came to a standstill in the highway and absorbed the beauty of this part of the country. I stepped out of the Hummer and tried to straighten the clothes I'd napped in. They had enough spandex to never wrinkle, regardless of what my job entailed.

I felt the smile race across my face as I remembered coming here as a young child with Mama before the Sunday she furnished the flowers for the church service. We would pick all the gladiolas we could pack in the trunk of her red Chevrolet. She always picked the end of summer when she knew Mr. Gaddy opened the fields to the public. We would get the flowers home, take all Saturday afternoon to pull off the spent ones, and separate the colors into tall buckets. Mama would cut the stalks to keep them from being top-heavy, and arrange vases of unforgettable combinations.

Early on Sunday morning, she and I would drive to the church and put the arrangements on the pulpit, then go home and dress for church. Mama enjoyed the compliments even though she didn't buy the flowers. My favorite Sunday coincided with Daddy's turn, as head deacon, to prepare all the little glasses of wine—actually grape juice—for the Atkinson Baptist Church communion service. He also had to cut tiny squares of white bread from the many long fresh loaves he'd bought for the occasion.

A tear appeared on my cheek and I wiped it away. I had some great memories of Daddy, who died of a massive heart attack, leaving all of us stunned. Fifty-years-old. I was only nine. Mama never remarried, and the overwhelming aroma of fresh bread and grape juice never again filled the house. We moved to Genesis Beach to be near Daddy's sister and her family. I shook my head to let these thoughts exit. I could stay in them all day, but I had serious work to do.

Even though the memory of Daddy temporarily slipped

back onto my mind's shelf, another surfaced. I still remembered milking my first cow in Mr. Green's dairy barn, not too many roads over. Fascinated by how the milk went from the warm cow's udder into vats in trucks to be hauled away and pasteurized, I could find nothing to compare to the taste of fresh milk straight from the cow.

Mr. Green had more patience than most people I'd ever met. Once when I came back from Genesis Beach to visit at the farm, spending the day with his children, he told me to hop on the tractor and drive it to the fence gate, and he'd open it. Reluctant to tell him I'd never driven a tractor, I hopped on and took off. Unfortunately, I got to the gate long before Mr. Green, and not knowing the difference between the clutch and brakes, I plowed right through it, tearing it right off its hinges.

It rattled me, but he didn't seem to be upset at all. Or, at least, he didn't let on. The fence had to be fixed before dark since the cows would surely find the opening and wander all over the country, and some into the highway.

I shook my head fitfully. *Here I go again.* I could have allowed more childhood memories to flood my mind, but I had to refocus and get on with the murder investigation.

A large pile of topsoil, banded with cottonseed waste from the county gin, waited for new plantings. I wondered if Mr. Gaddy still lived around here. He'd be in his late eighties. I didn't see any movement around the house. He had always been a kind man, and he didn't even get angry when I acquired my driver's license, and Mama and I drove up here to visit Daddy's brother, my Uncle Clarence. A forest fire, a few miles down the road, got my attention and Mama and I both looked that way. Out of nowhere, Mr. Gaddy's two big dogs, a collie and a German police dog, ran into the road. I hit them both, killing them instantly. I stopped and cried and apologized, but Mr. Gaddy consoled me. Mama wouldn't let me drive the rest of the way, though that was one of the few times I ever saw her tremble.

I shook my head hard enough to dislocate it. *I really have to stop reminiscing and get on with my investigation!*

With one last glance at the place, I headed down Hoe Road, following the directions Edsel Foxx gave me to Hound Dog Road. I took a left and bumped down the dirt path that seemed to have hundreds of bottomless holes, easing toward a gray doublewide with dark blue shutters and a wood deck. A wooden sign across the front door read: *The Foxx Den.* The trailer, rather plain and short, had pale siding, the roof just a tad darker, and shutters several shades darker than that. Two puny bushes, planted in the front yard seemed to be volunteers, not planted with any landscape design in mind. The yard consisted of more weeds than anything else. Not much to mow. A gray Japanese lantern decorated the yard.

I approached the porch as a spider web latched onto me. I hadn't seen it even though its exceeding thickness enveloped my shoulder and swaddled my ear. I squirmed with uneasiness because I figured a monstrous, hairy spider came with the package.

Relieved to see Mr. Foxx stepping out, I swept the web from around me.

"The spiders are terrible around here. How ya doing? Your timing's perfect," he said, handing me a glass of sweet tea. "Let's sit out here, if you don't mind. My girlfriend's still sleeping."

I sat in the upholstered swing after he plopped on the chaise lounge.

"Thank you for being so cooperative. The sooner I get this done, the better, but I do need to read you your rights." He looked quizzical. "It's just a precautionary measure to protect you, Mr. Foxx."

"No problem. I haven't done anything wrong, so it don't bother me. Like I said, Agent Hunter, Nita and I got drunk and got married. We'd kinda been flirting around some, but I certainly had no interest in marrying her. My God, she's at least fifteen years older than me."

"I'm more interested in learning all I can about Clara Banoak. Fill me in."

He put his freckled right index finger to his red head and smiled. I noticed the dimples for the first time. His gorgeous eyes matched his shirt, and he appeared to be closer to my age than to Nita's. *Is he flirting with me?* I cleared my throat.

"Mr. Foxx..."

"Sly. Nobody calls me Mr. Foxx. I go by Sly."

I bet you do. "Okay. I've got it, thanks. Tell me all you can about Clara Banoak and anyone who might want to hurt her." I fished the PDA from my breast pocket and flipped it open.

"You gonna record this?"

"If you don't mind."

He chuckled. "Hell, I don't mind. But you're fixing to have some choice words from me about that woman. To be blunt, Agent Hunter, Clara Banoak was a hateful bitch. We kids used to have a joke about her having rabies. She could get so mad she literally foamed at the mouth, or at least it seemed that way when I was a teenager."

"How long have you known her?"

"All my life. She lived in that fancy house when I first heard about her. My daddy hates her too. He used to hunt. All the hunters despise her. She got worse after her husband died, acting like the hunters threw gasoline on her. They minded their own business and if they talked about her at all, it was over at Yonder Store, not to her face. She'd get newspapers and cut out pictures of any hunters with a deer or a bear, or even rabbits and gobblers, and write something mean on the edge of it and mail it."

"Did she ever send you a picture?"

"No, but she sent my daddy one. You can't talk to him though. He had a stroke at forty-five and is in a rest home. He can hear but he can't talk or write, so it's pointless. I'm gonna tell him she's dead, though. He'll be happy."

I pulled my shoulders back.

"I reckon you think I'm callous. I'm sorry somebody gutted her, but I'm not sorry she's dead. Anybody tells you they're sorry, Agent Hunter, you need to check them out real good." His tone was now anything but charming.

"Where were you the night of the murder, Mr. Foxx?"

"I do shift work, like I told you at Yonder Store. I go in at eleven and get off at eight in the morning. Then I come home and sleep a while."

"You work all night long?"

"Yep. You can verify that with the company. I punch a time card. I even did about forty minutes of overtime."

I stood.

"I appreciate your cooperation and candor, Mr...Sly. If you overhear anything about this case, please let me know." I clicked *Off* on the recorder, and gave him my card and the glass, now clanking with melting ice.

"Agent Hunter, I'll be surprised if you get much help with this case. I'm telling you, people here are glad she's dead, and they thank whoever did it."

"Mr. Foxx?"

"Yes?"

"Would you tell me if you knew who did it?" A smile slid across his face.

"Yes, ma'am, but begrudgingly, and only because I don't want a murderer living around here." At least he seemed honest about his feelings. "And besides, being interviewed by an agent as foxy as you is no problem at all." I knew I blushed.

Four o'clock, two hours before I could talk with Acme Beavers, I left the Foxx Den and drove to Yonder Store in the fork of the road and got a bottle of water and a suspicious-looking Moon Pie, my only choice. I headed down Register Road and met Ogden Gunn. We pulled over on the shoulders and got out.

"There wasn't one clear print on the skinner. 'Course it don't really surprise me. Whoever killed Clara wasn't stupid."

I told him what Sly Foxx said and he concurred. "Yep, people here aren't apt to open up, especially to SBI. It might take months for somebody to get loose lips and start bragging. Probably won't do it while you're around, I'm sorry to say."

I shrugged. "I'm going to question the other folks on my list anyway, and maybe you and I can come up with a plan, or a reward to get the lips loose sooner."

He nodded.

We decided to ride back to the crime scene and go over the house and grounds again while we had some time. We swung into the back gravel driveway and parked inside the white fence. Together we walked toward the back porch, and I angled off to the old weathered shed. I considered a sign above the door that read: *Boston Whales, 1875*. Sheriff Gunn headed over to me.

"This is an interesting sign. Certainly is out of place here, wouldn't you say?"

"Mr. Banoak collected old signs and stuff. The artist in him, I reckon. Folk art mostly. He'd find junk and paint it into some fine piece of art. I'm sure he thought that shed was a good place for this sign he found somewhere. He liked to go antiquing. He never went to sea though, at least not that I know of."

"So there's no story behind the sign?"

"Not that I'm aware of. Just a vacation souvenir," the sheriff said.

"What I'm hearing is Clara behaved better before he died. Did you know him?"

"Yes'm. Eli Banoak was a fine man. A man of character. Soft-spoken. Never a cross word about anybody. He kept her in line most of the time. He sure had his hands full, I reckon. She was an animal activist even back then. Him too, but he wasn't mean and unreasonable about it. He got involved if somebody starved an animal or something like that, but he understood hunting, and how overpopulation and starvation can be a worse way for an animal to die. Clara? Now she reacted. It didn't take much to set her off."

We moved toward the house and the sheriff introduced me to the department's only detective, Billy Horrell. Gunn and I entered through the kitchen while Horrell moved on around the outside of the house. The kitchen looked the same. We discussed the fact she must have gone to the front door and opened it to her murderer. The same questions kept reappearing. Did she know him, or them? Why had she let them in? No sign of forced entry on any door, and the front door had no marks to indicate she'd tried to slam it or that it had been kicked in.

Detective Horrell walked in. "Sheriff Gunn, Agent Hunter, you might want to take a look at what I've found in the front bushes." We followed Horrell, who pulled back some boxwood so we could see a white spotlight.

"What's your theory, Detective?"

"Right off-hand, I'd say it could have been used to blind her when she opened the door. The candlepower is two million. That would explain how he got in and on her without a struggle."

I looked at Gunn.

He nodded. "Sounds reasonable."

"Do both of you think this was a one-man operation?"

"Could have been with the gambrel. And she's so teeny," Horrell said.

I tried to explain my thoughts. "That would mean holding the spotlight, blinding her, overpowering her, gutting her, and mounting her on the gambrel. That's a lot for one person to handle."

"Lemmie ought to know by now if she died before the gutting. I certainly hope so," Horrell said.

"But, you're right, Agent Hunter. That's a lot, unless he came in and bonked her on the head to subdue her," Gunn responded.

I got my evidence kit, put on gloves, examined the spotlight, and soon found an ideal fingerprint, every tiny line unsmeared, as if left deliberately for me to find. With my magnifying glass I followed the human road map that encircled circles, ending at the tip of the finger. I bagged and labeled the spotlight.

"Good work, Horrell," I said. The detective tipped his hat and wandered across the yard. Ogden Gunn took the downstairs and I worked my way upstairs, avoiding the dried red blotches. At the top I walked to the center of the rail and looked down. I checked the rail for scratches. Streaks of blood were smeared right above the foyer light fixture. My theory that she'd been lifted over and dropped still made sense to me. The chandelier in the center of the foyer was substantial, but it only stayed attached because of Clara's small size. More than likely, a larger person would have caused the light fixture to pull away from the ceiling.

I figured once split open, she was hoisted over the edge of the balcony, and the entrails dropped out, making an inconceivable mess on the floor below.

A display for added drama?

Premeditated. No doubt about that.

Well-planned, yes.

Horrendous beyond words.

A hunter's retaliation? Or had hunters been made the scapegoats?

I opened the door behind me and walked across the bedroom to another door. I looked at the front yard and the river, not too far over the bedroom's balcony rail, where Horrell snooped around like a bird dog, his nose pointed toward the ground and his keister pointed upward. I checked the door and the balcony rails, but there were no signs that anyone climbed over them. I continued to work my way around the area and back into the room, glancing at my watch.

I dialed the SBI lab and asked for Wiley Savage.

"Agent Hunter, I was about to call you."

"Good. You got something for me?"

"No. Every bit of the lab evidence I collected is Clara Banoak's. I got nothing from the killer or anyone else. Sorry I couldn't have been more helpful."

"You did your best. If he—or they—wore gloves, that pretty

much knocks out any prints. I hoped maybe one of them got cut, threw up, or left some DNA behind."

"No such luck. Oh, I tested the cigarette you bagged. I couldn't find a match for the print on it. Sorry I don't have any good news."

I had already figured out the cigarette belonged to Nita Quicki. Clara Banoak didn't smoke. I thanked him and headed out the door.

I would have to leave for my appointment with Mr. Beavers, so I found the sheriff and told him I'd see him tomorrow.

Four

I reached Buckskin Crossroads and stopped just in time to watch a yellow and gray pickup with a rusty bed race by. The man driving had a head full of long white hair blowing in the breeze. He grinned at me as he passed. Cyrano Blood. It had to be. He looked like a lunatic. His face full of large teeth made him resemble a hairy piranha. I didn't look forward to meeting him. His back bumper sticker read: *The Lone Ranger Rides Again.*

I turned left and stared at the sun retreating through the trees, making the rest of the universe lavender, the most splendid, soothing hue I'd ever seen. I took several curves before seeing "Beavers" written on a mailbox. I drove in and parked beside a barking chocolate lab that either came to greet me or to take off my leg. A man with a toothpick wiggling in his mouth appeared at the door of the small, one-story white house with a high-pitched roof.

"Chester, get back here!" he yelled. The dog sauntered off with his tail between his legs.

"Mr. Beavers? I'm Logan Hunter, SBI." I flashed my badge.

A woman and three children appeared at the door. A teen-aged boy stepped out, saying something about the Hummer.

"Come on in, Agent Hunter. I heard you coming." Acme Beavers was more like an auburn-haired grizzly than a beaver, overweight, but not by much. His chin looked as if a golf ball had been surgically implanted under the skin. His complexion—a linebacker had ran across his face with metal cleats. And even then, not a bad-looking man. Not handsome, either.

"You young'uns leave the Hummer alone now."

"It's okay, really. They can look it over. I have the keys," I assured him. They ran past us and circled it, making loud oohs and ahs. Mr. Beavers held the door as I walked into the foyer, dirty with plenty of handprints, and into the great room. The light hardwood floor matched the beams in the pitched ceiling, and video games and piles of newspapers covered most of it.

Mr. Beavers offered me the worn dark red sofa and he pulled a chair over from the corner table, still sucking on the toothpick. Mrs. Beavers disappeared into the kitchen after greeting me.

"I guess you know why I'm here, Mr. Beavers."

"Acme. I feel old enough without being called mister. And, yeah, I reckon I do, Agent Hunter. That's an awful thing to hear about Clara. Everbody hated her, but no one deserves that."

"Do you hunt, Acme?"

"Does a bear have claws?"

I laughed. "So I suppose you and Clara had your share of run-ins?"

"Not so much. In the beginning, we did. Years ago. But then I started going out west to hunt. I never wanted my picture in the papers, and I still never tell where the game is. I'm private, I reckon. And selfish. I like to keep my good spots to myself. She left me pretty much alone."

"Who did she hound the most?"

"Generally, the deer hunters, I think. Her main targets. And they're usually the ones who want their pictures in the paper with their trophy deer, so they became easy targets. Most of the deer hunters around here have problems with her every deer season."

"Can you give me some names?"

"I could probably give you a few names, but you have to understand. Men come from all over this part of the state to hunt around here. The possibilities are endless. She didn't bother the bird hunters much though. She went after big-game hunters mostly. Deer, bear, elk, moose. Even coyotes. Sometimes there would be a turkey hunter in the paper, but I don't know if she set out to get them.

"You might want to check the newspapers. *The Wilmington Star* archives might have a few pictures. She'd sign her name to those threats she'd write and mail them to the hunter. You ask Hawk Daw. I bet he's still got the picture. His son, Ethan, killed his first deer, and Hawk put it in the paper. She mailed the picture and told the boy he ought to be killed. People don't take kindly to that sort of thing." He fumbled with a pillow near his elbow. "Some of the hunters got to her real good one Sunday though."

"How's that?"

"Clara always went to church. So the Sunday after Ethan Daw got that threat in the mail, fifteen or twenty hunters got in the balcony of the church and stared at her. She pretty much stared them down. She could intimidate as good as anybody I ever met."

"What church is that?"

"This one right down this road out here," he said, taking the deteriorating toothpick from his hairy lips. "Cross the bridge and you'll see it. It's old and tiny, but they still have services there. It'll seat more than you might expect. There's a balcony runs down both sides. They say slaves used to sit up there while their masters worshiped below."

"Were you one of the hunters who tried to antagonize her?"

"Yes, I have to admit it." He took off his nasty cap and threw it on an end table. "But you gotta understand, Agent Hunter. The hunters aren't the bad guys in all this."

"Where were you the night of the gutting, Mr. Beavers?"

"I took off work that day, and me and Rachel Blanche took the young'uns and went to Wilmington. They're outgrowing their clothes. We stayed down there the whole day. We ate out. I reckon she's still got the receipts if you need to see 'em."

"About what time did you get home?"

"Oh, I reckon about ten o'clock."

"Did you go out again?"

"No. We all got baths and hit the sack. I had to be at work early the next morning."

"Thank you for the information. And, for what it's worth, I'm not taking sides. I have to be objective and get the facts. I'm not passing judgment on anybody. I appreciate your time, sir. Thank you for your candor. If you think of anything else, please call me. Here's a card with all my numbers."

Mrs. Beavers stepped into the room with her apron on. "Supper's ready."

"Do you want to stay for supper, Agent Hunter?"

"It smells wonderful, but I have another appointment. Thanks for your time."

"You'd better change your mind. Rachel Blanche cooks the best possum and sweet potato casserole you ever tasted."

I had somewhere else I wanted to be, thank goodness.

I checked my voicemail back in the Hummer. Lemmie Sawyer had left the message I'd been waiting for. Clara Banoak died before the gutting took place. He based his theory on a stab wound to her chest not consistent with the gutting line. He couldn't pinpoint the actual time of death, but guessed between seven at night and two the next morning. He said her stomach contents indicated that she hadn't eaten supper. Apparently the killer or killers stabbed her and then created all the drama to drive home a point. No pun intended.

I located Cyrano Blood's house, modern with an immaculate yard. A contradiction to the man I'd seen earlier. What little I'd glimpsed of him certainly couldn't be considered neat—one of the hairiest men I'd ever seen. I stepped out of the Hummer to peek around a little. I didn't see his old truck, and the big hound dog chained to a stake in the yard appeared to be sleeping.

I'd parked down a path between the third and fourth rows of mature blueberry bushes in the field, hoping the unique copper color wouldn't be noticed over the bush tops I used as camouflage. I checked around the yard, but really wanted to get inside the house or the red barn near it. I kept one eye on the dog as I eased into the yard. I sidled up to the house and peeked through a window into the den. Neat with everything in place. A wood-beam mantle stood out in an otherwise white room. Three pitchfork tines posed on its top.

I heard the old rattletrap truck coming up the dirt path and darted behind a pine tree before sprinting for the field. The sun disappeared and one stray cloud's bladder emptied on me.

Soaked, and with little time to spare before going to Hawk Daw's again, I grabbed the towel I kept in the Hummer, mopped my hair, and patted down my clothes, switching the air on high to dry out.

Five

Hawk Daw met me at the door and motioned me in. "I'd invite you to sit on the porch, but the skeeters would eat us both alive." I thanked him for his thoughtfulness. He motioned me to the navy leather couch and he sat back in his Barcalounger and picked up a glass.

"Oh, I'm sorry. Let me fix you a drink," he said, lowering his chair.

"No, please. I'm fine, Mr. Daw." I pulled out my PDA. "I'd just like to ask you a few questions about the Banoak case and I'll go."

He eyed me.

"Where you from, Detective?"

"It's agent, Agent Hunter. I'm from Genesis Beach, over two hours away, but the bureau sends me all over the state."

"You drive back and forth, do ya?"

"It depends. I did the first night on this case. I thought about staying at The Azalea Motel, but changed my mind."

He laughed. "Thank God for that. At least you've got some sense. I think it's about to fall in."

"Yeah, I rode by and looked at the place. They're renovating, and it looks like it'll be nice once they finish. I don't think I could stand all the hammering and sawing, although I might be too tired to care by the time I put my head on a pillow. It has been an incredibly long day."

"Well, if you ever need a place to rest your head, you're

welcome to stay with us. It's just my son and me."

We both sat in silence for a moment. "I appreciate the offer to stay here, but that would be very awkward. Besides, I hope this is a quick case. I've got wedding plans to make."

"You think this'll be an easy case? You must already have a suspect."

"If truth be told, no. It's just wishful thinking on my part, I guess."

He nodded.

"I have way too many suspects. I need to be able to eliminate most of them." I cleared my throat and gave him the spiel about rights. He agreed to talk since he said he had no reason to hide anything.

"Mr. Daw, I understand you've had some trouble with Clara Banoak. I believe your son's name came up."

His mustache twitched. His smile went elsewhere. I struck a nerve.

He got out of his chair and went to what appeared to be a bedroom door and closed it. He brushed his fingers through his mustache. "I'd rather not have Ethan hear this conversation. He's fifteen. He started hunting with me about three years ago. He'd been sitting in stands with me for years, and at that point I figured he was old enough to have a real gun. I taught him all the safety rules for hunting before I bought it, in case you think that's early."

"No, not at all. Mr. Daw..."

"Please call me Hawk. Formality scares me. Especially with an SBI agent."

"Okay, Hawk. Tell me what you hunt and how Clara Banoak got involved."

"I've hunted all my life. I started as young as Ethan. Just about all the men around here hunt. Deer mostly. But a few of the locals go off on big-game hunts to Nebraska, Montana, or Texas. Acme Beavers goes about every year. He's even been to Canada on a moose hunt.

"Anyway, I'd occasionally bag a big buck, you know, eight or ten points and a sizable body. I reckon it's kinda asinine, but most of us enjoy bragging about the big ones. It's proof if you've got a picture. When I was about nineteen, the old bitch...'scuse me, ma'am, but I hated her guts." His face reddened. "I mean it. I'm not gone mince words. I'm sorry she was gutted, and that was a poor choice of words, but I hated her. So did everybody else around here if they're honest with you."

I leaned forward. "What did she do to make you hate her so much?"

He picked up his glass. "Last chance to order a drink, Agent Hunter." I shook my head as he headed for the kitchen.

"Listen, have you had any supper? I haven't. Let me fix us a steak and you can meet Ethan. You've gotta eat, right? And one drink ain't gonna hurt you. I'll let you make it."

"No, I couldn't." Hunger gnawed at the back of my ribcage. "I shouldn't," I added in a less than convincing voice.

He turned and smiled. "I insist. Bet you haven't had much to eat since you got here. Am I right?"

"Yep. I haven't found the deli yet."

His laughter filled the room.

"The best you can do around here is get a freezer, drive thirty miles to the biggest grocery store in the county, and get enough to last a month."

"I've noticed that Yonder Store's about the only place to even get a stale sandwich."

"Yonder Store's okay for soft drinks, toilet paper, and charcoal, but don't buy bread and milk there. They spoil between deliveries. It's not Mitchell's fault."

That must be Navel Face.

"He has a huge farm and really doesn't need the store. He reopened it to help out those of us who don't want to drive thirty miles for little crap all the time." He looked up and smiled. "I'm fixing you a first-rate meal. No brag, just fact. I know it's late, but we usually eat late during crop season."

That sounded good to me. With nowhere to get anything, even stale food, I nodded agreement and joined him in the kitchen, hoping he wasn't the murderer with intent to poison me. I felt surprisingly comfortable with him so far, but I had no intention of letting my guard down.

"Get the blueberries out of the fridge, please. They ought to be thawed by now. I'll show you how to make a delicious cobbler, quick and easy." He grinned. "It's been a long time since we had a woman in the kitchen." Hawk pulled out four steaks from the freezer and shoved them into the microwave to defrost.

Four steaks?

He picked up a plastic grocery bag of fresh okra and dumped it into the sink before walking to the bedroom door and saying something I couldn't understand to his son.

He headed for the back door and turned. "He'll be out once he finishes his homework. And I'm going out to light the grill. Be right back."

I found ingredients for the cobbler, rinsed the berries, and located a knife to snip the ends off the late-season okra. The berries drained in a colander and I'd just completed my snipping when Hawk reappeared. I selected two eggs from inside of the refrigerator door, and as the cracked one slipped through my fingers, I tried to corral the uncorralable. The egg hit the floor and spattered in all directions, the yolk bleeding yellow over the floor tiles. I made squeaky noises as Hawk Daw ran for paper towels and salt.

"Here, let me." He sprinkled a good amount of salt on the mess and cleaned up the floor in an instant. "I've had practice with eggs." He smiled.

"Thanks, I guess you can tell I don't cook much."

"I'd imagine you're on the road too much for that." I nodded. "I didn't mean to be gone so long. I had trouble lighting the charcoal."

Or has he been out sabotaging the Hummer or something worse?

He instructed me to cut the okra into wheels for frying, which made me happy. It had been a long time since I'd eaten fresh fried okra. My mouth watered. He presented me with a drink and started on the cobbler as the microwave bell indicated thawed steaks.

"How do you manage to have okra this late in the fall?"

"I've got a garden out back. Ethan and I both love the stuff. It stays tender as long as I keep it cut. Some of the stalks are taller than I am. But the frost will get it any day now, and it'll be over until next year. It's been nice to have a warm fall though."

"What else is planted there?"

"That's all that's left. The butterbeans died and the tomatoes are over. The cukes are long gone. I'd intended to plant some fall peas, but never got around to it. The farm crops have to come first."

"Mr. Daw, do you mind if I ask you what happened to your wife?"

"Not at all. I went up north and married a city girl when I worked for an electric company. When I was ready to move back home, she gave up her job and came too, looking forward to a little country adventure. It didn't take her long to miss Cleveland. She liked convenience and fresh markets all around her. Here, well, like I said earlier, you have to drive thirty miles to get a fresh loaf of bread. She just didn't fit in.

"She packed up and left one Saturday while I was in the woods hunting. She left a note to tell me she'd left Ethan, who was about one and a half, with a neighbor. That boiled my ass. I charged her with abandonment and got full custody. It's pretty much just been the two of us ever since. She never calls or sends him presents."

"I'm sorry."

"Don't be. It's the best thing that could've happened. I got rid of her and got a great son. We're doing just fine without her."

I smiled.

"Getting back to our conversation, I had my picture in the

paper with one of the biggest deer ever killed in these parts. I was nineteen. Clara cornered my pa at Yonder Store and told him I was a killer and that we both ought to be shot. My pa laid into her with every cuss word he knew. I just stood there in shock. I'd never seen anybody act like that in my life. She was our enemy after that."

"That had to be many years ago."

"Do you mean what took me so long to kill her?" Now nose-to-nose with me, his whole demeanor changed in an instant.

I gulped. "No, that's not what I meant at all. You're unquestionably defensive, Mr. Daw." I put down my paring knife. "I think I'd better go. We'll talk again, in a more formal setting."

"No. No, Agent Hunter," he said in a kinder voice. "I'm sorry. I guess I'm on edge. I know you came here to question me and I guess I feel like a suspect."

"Should you be?"

"Damn if I know! You're here for a reason. That much I know."

"I'm here because Clara Banoak had a problem with your son, Mr. Daw." He blinked at me and handed me the knife.

"Okay. Let's start over. Go ahead and ask."

"How did you handle things after she confronted you and your father?"

"There was nothing to handle for a couple of years. Then I had my picture in the paper again. I went with Acme on a trip and killed a non-typical mule deer. They're much bigger than our white tails. Anyway, I couldn't resist. Acme was in the picture too. She sent him the picture with a nasty note about us. He told me about it, but I didn't want to see it. I knew it would piss me off.

"And yes, I suppose I am defensive. Somebody whacks the old bitty and now I'm a suspect."

"I never said you're a suspect. I have to question people, and the only lead I have right now is that the murder victim was strung up on a gambrel used for skinning deer, Mr. Daw, and she was gutted like a deer. We found a spotlight, like hunters use, outside in her front bushes, but we haven't determined whose prints are on it."

We both turned as the bedroom door opened and a handsome young man walked out wearing rumpled khaki shorts and a Bass Pro Shop tee shirt. A tiny girl with pale skin and ink-black hair, dyed, no doubt, followed him like a shadow.

"Agent Hunter, this is Ethan, my son."

The teen, who looked much older than fifteen, walked over and shook my hand.

"Agent Hunter's an SBI agent." The boy looked puzzled. "The SBI is the state equivalent of the feds."

The boy's eyes brightened and his grip grew stronger. He looked at his father. "Dad, is everything all right? You all got kinda loud out here."

"Everything's fine, son."

Ethan turned back to me. "I've never met a real agent. Are you here about old lady Banoak?" The teenager spoke with an unusually deep and husky voice.

Hawk gave his son a hard look. "Don't be disrespectful now, Ethan."

"But, Dad, you said she deserved it."

Hawk turned red again.

"And this is Lilith Hufstickle." The girl stood still, not uttering a word.

"Check on the steaks, buddy. We want them a little pink in the middle, right, Agent Hunter?"

Ethan and Lilith headed out the door as I nodded.

"I reckon I'm guilty of saying that, for sure. It's funny how the things you say to a kid in passing come back to haunt you." He looked over at me. "Do you think I killed her?"

"Did you?" I looked him dead in the eyes and never blinked.

"No. But I wanted to after Ethan killed his deer last New Year's Day."

"Another ugly confrontation?"

"Yeah. A passive confrontation, I guess you'd call it. She cut out his picture with the deer, a nice one, and mailed it to him personally. I guess she figured he wouldn't show it to me, but he did." The door opened and the teens came in with the steaks. "Let's eat. We can talk later."

We enjoyed our meal, the best one I'd had in a while. Ethan told me about basketball camp and the trophy he'd won on the final day. "You're so tall, for a woman, I mean. I know you played basketball, didn't you?"

I winced. "Believe it or not, only one year. My freshman year. I was a total klutz, fouling out in five minutes. I rode the pines, most of the time. I often wonder why the coach didn't just tell me to take a hike. I was a total spaz!"

Ethan grinned and wolfed down some steak. Hawk sat back in his chair, watching his son and I interact. Lilith Hufstickle had not said a word. She made me feel a little uncomfortable. Or maybe I unintentionally made *her* feel that way. Whichever, she gave me the creeps. Pretty enough, but she reminded me too much of Morticia from The Addams Family television re-runs I'd watched as a child. Right down to her black fingernails. Her eyes looked sunk in with all the atrociously heavy mascara. Her demeanor was just as disturbing.

"Did you try any more sports?"

"Yeah, as a matter of fact I did, if you call cheering a sport. I was, by far, the tallest one on the squad."

"How'd you do?"

"All-conference three years in a row."

"Wow!" Ethan seemed to be impressed, but quickly changed the subject. I wanted to engage Lilith in the conversation, but I never got a chance. "Dad, since I've got my permit, can Lilith and I drive to the bridge and back? I won't be gone long."

Hawk glanced at his son. "Now, Ethan, you know I have to ride with you, and Agent Hunter is interviewing me right now. Maybe tomorrow," he said, patting his son's arm.

"Aw shucks! It's not far."

"Sorry, Ethan," wasn't much of a consolation to the boy.

Once we'd finished the main meal, Hawk brought the blueberry cobbler out with a scoop of vanilla-bean ice cream on top.

"This is wonderful. And I like this crust better than most."

"It's just white bread with the crust trimmed off. My aunt gave me this recipe. We love it, don't we, Ethan? We throw in peaches, strawberries, whatever's in season or looks good at the super market."

I'd have to tell Pepper about it.

Once we'd completed the meal, we all walked into the den.

"Ethan, go get the note. The one Ms. Banoak sent you." Ethan hesitated until Hawk gave him a little shove. Lilith followed him. We both found seats, and when they returned, he handed it to me:

Ethan Daw,
You're a murderer!
You're a killer!
You hurt poor defenseless animals!
You should be shot!

I looked over the ugly scrawl of a bright red felt-tip penned signature where she'd blatantly signed her name.

"I can see how this would make you angry."

Hawk motioned Ethan and Lilith back to the bedroom. "Wind up the homework, son. It's time for Lilith to go home."

The door closed behind the two without another word.

"I don't want him involved any more than he has to be. He was mighty upset. He didn't sleep for weeks. Didn't hunt neither. How she could do that to a kid? It infuriated me. But, Agent Hunter, I swear to you I didn't kill her. If I was gone do it, it would have been in January, right after we got this. You can see the date at the top. I didn't do it."

I wanted to believe him.

"How about Acme? Mr. Foxx? Or Cyrano Blood?"

"You'd have to ask them. I don't think Sly is capable of anything like this, and he's mainly a wing nut anyway."

"A wing nut?"

"Yeah, an avid bird hunter."

"O…kay. So, do they call deer hunters doe nuts?"

Daw laughed. "Not that I know of, but that's a good one." He cleared his throat and got serious again.

"I don't think Acme would do it either, Agent Hunter, even though he's kinda strange. Now Cyrano? He's registered crazy. He's a dextro head. I wouldn't put anything past him, but I didn't just say that. Please don't use my name. I don't want him over here in my face."

I promised. "You've been more than kind. I appreciate your time and the delicious meal. Tell Ethan I enjoyed meeting him. And I just have one more question."

"What's that?"

"What's a dextro head?"

"He drinks Nyquil and other cough syrups like soft drinks. He's addicted to that mess."

"I've heard of people hooked on cough syrup, but uggh! Nyquil tastes pretty awful!" I walked down the steps and turned to face the man. "I may have more questions later."

"Come back any time, Agent Hunter."

"Oh, one more question. Where were you the night Clara Banoak died?"

"We've been trying hard to get all the crops in, and we've stayed in the field from sun up to past sun-down. Then I take the crops to market, or wherever they're going."

"Can anybody vouch for your whereabouts the entire night?"

"All my crew. But most of them don't speak English."

Hawk watched me from the door as I fought my way through carnivorous bugs to the Hummer.

Six

After a night of uninterrupted sleep in my own bed, I drove back to the house not far from Beatty's Bridge with a biscuit and large chai tea latte I purchased on the way. I staked out Cyrano Blood, parking the Hummer in the blueberry bushes again, not sure I wanted to be alone with him. Not that I was afraid of him. What then? All the gossip I'd heard about him was unflattering, but then, were the gossipers credible, or trying to turn my focus away from themselves?

When he appeared on horseback from the other side of the blueberry field near his house, I had no time to react. He clearly knew I was there. His broad smile made me think of an old grizzly that had cornered its supper. Hawk called him crazy. He looked it. The gun in my ankle pocket made me brave enough to step out and acknowledge him.

"Mr. Blood."

He brought his horse, a magnificent beast, up beside me and thrust out his hand. A strong shake.

"Agent Hunter. Why'd you park an Army tank in my blueberry field?" Before I could answer, he continued. "I've been expecting you to question me, and you haven't."

His bluntness caught me off guard.

"I've been questioning a lot of folks. Just getting to you, sir."

He grinned.

"No time like the present. Follow me and I'll saddle up Sis for you." He trotted off down the side of the field before I could decline his offer.

Alone with him on horses?

I couldn't imagine any way this could be good. Not sensible at all. But if I didn't follow him, he'd think I was scared of him, and I wasn't. After all I did have my gun, didn't I?

I drove up to Mr. Blood's barn and reluctantly got out. I hadn't ridden a horse since my tenth birthday, and that fleabag bit me on the back of my arm once I got off.

Bloody hell! I have to think of a way out of this. I was sweating bullets.

Mr. Blood walked Sis out of the barn, already saddled for me. He grinned again, making me nervous. "Saddle up, Missy. We won't ride for long, and Sis is gentle." He mounted and waited for me.

"Mr. Blood, I'm not riding this horse!" He grinned, pulled his horse's reins a little to the side and started down a sandy path, never looking back at me.

Damn it!

I sashayed to the horse and patted her long head. I said a few sweet things in her ear, and she cut her eyes at me. With a long sigh, I threw my long leg over the horse, and, much to my surprise, landed in the saddle. I caught up with Blood's horse and we walked side by side at a slow gait. I didn't look at the man because I knew he had to be snickering.

He soon started the conversation, rubbing his nose, which resembled a bull's hairy gonad. And I knew about that subject. I'd once seen a bull's family jewels up close and personal. Too close and too personal.

"I know I'm a suspect. Like all the rest. I used to deer hunt, but that got boring. I moved up to bear. We have some around here, you know."

I must have looked shaken, my groin already rubbing on the saddle. I knew I'd be sore.

"Clara must have had lots of enemies."

"You betcha," he replied, picking up speed. I couldn't read his eyes. They seemed either sad or suspicious, angling down at the sides just below his bushy brows, which were darker than his white hair and mostly pepper mustache. Sis insisted on staying with his horse so I had no choice as I bounced up and down while she trotted.

"If you'll relax, you won't be so raw once we're through. You aren't a rider."

I felt no need to comment.

"People say I'm crazy—and I'm quite sure you've already been told that. But Clara Banoak was the crazy one. I seldom bother other people. I keep to myself most of the time when I'm not at work. I enjoy my farm and my horses. I don't go off prying into other people's business—and that's about all she did. She stayed in somebody's business all the time—her favorite past-time, especially after Eli died."

He sounded intelligent, but I kept both eyes on him, letting him spill his guts. Questions didn't seem necessary. He picked up more speed and Sis went too. Even though I tried to hold her back, she paid no attention to me.

We trotted along for about a mile and the two horses turned onto another sandy path that went back through another blueberry field. Although my legs were long, my thighs ached from being spread so far apart. Sis was certainly full-grown. Blood's horse settled into a gallop and Sis copied. I gritted my teeth each time I hit the saddle—hard. I turned to ask Blood if he had an alibi the night of the murder, but I never got the chance.

Sis reared.

"Hang on tight!" Cyrano Blood yelled at me. "Snake!"

Sis angled and took off full speed. I dug my heels in and hung on to the reins with all the strength I could muster. She wouldn't halt for me. I had to let her run until she stopped on her own. Some distance back, I could see Blood coming behind us. Sis bolted through the field and to the edge near Blood's property.

She took a quick left and I went straight, landing face first in the white sand and ditch briars. I looked up to see Sis heading for the barn.

Blood dismounted and reached for me. "Agent Hunter, I'm so sorry. I do apologize. It wasn't my intention to hurt you or to piss you off."

I ignored his hand and got up by myself. I dusted off and started walking gingerly toward the barn. I learned nothing. Zero. Nada. Zilch. My crotch hurt, and I was, indeed, pissed off.

"Mr. Blood, I'll be seeing you again, but on my own terms," I announced, glaring at his saccharine smirk.

It disappeared instantly.

"Call me Cy. Let me take care of those scratches. I need to make this up to you. How about supper?"

"Hell no!" I waddled toward the Hummer. Yep, Mr. Smart Ass would be seeing more of me. And I *did* think he meant to piss me off.

My butt and thighs throbbed. My scratches stung. And I didn't smell so good. Even though it was not even noon, I drove back to the beach, anger smoldering every time I hit a pothole along the way. I wanted to soak my backside in a long luxurious bath and doctor my scratches. Walking the beach and going to bed early seemed like a good plan.

Cyrano Blood wanted to intimidate? Well, he'll find out what I'm made of. I'm rough and tough and hard to bluff. I'll stand up to anybody, especially when I have my guns.

I'd have both my Ruger and my ankle gun from now on. I didn't trust any of those damn people.

As I approached the Genesis Beach Marina road, my cell phone rang. "Agent Hunter?"

"Yes. Sheriff Gunn?"

"Remember that fine fingerprint you found?"

"Sure."

"There's no doubt about who it belongs to."

"Well, are you going to make me beg?"

"Oh, sorry. That stunning fingerprint belongs to none other than Hawk Daw."

Hawk? Had I eaten supper with the murderer?

My skin crawled at the thought as I drove to Hawk Daw's house the next morning and rapped on the door. I wanted an explanation for his print on the spotlight found in Clara Banoak's shrubbery. Nobody answered my pounding on the door. At that point I realized that both trucks were gone.

I'd decided to skip a morning run on the beach and run when I got back to the country instead, so maybe I could clear my head and then find Hawk. The straight road from the Banoak house to the fork near Yonder Store provided a good place to run with little traffic. My head was filled with thoughts and a mass of jumbled data I needed to file somewhere in my mind. I often figured things out while running—like whether Hawk killed Clara Banoak. And if he had, why did he wait until now?

I found a path near the river that provided a more strenuous run, over protruding knobby roots, and uneven ground. I ran to Yonder Store and back, and cut onto the path, keeping my eyes peeled for anything that might be out of place, or a snake that hadn't realized winter loomed.

Bright yellow Golden Elf raised their leaves toward the sun, and some river shrubs filled with orangish blooms beginning to pop open, put on a show of their own. It surprised me to see fragrant Iron Bone blooming at this time of year. I enjoyed running and discovering along the way. I'd made a point to learn more about flowers after I realized how little I knew about them. Through research, I learned what flowers and plants to expect during each season, and when something didn't fit in the landscape. Sometimes a body found in the open yielded foliage or soil evidence that had been moved from the killing place to another location.

I enjoyed the peacefulness and stillness near the river, with a faint breeze every once in a while to keep me from sweating profusely. From above, I could see the river snaking its way along the banks, its water the highest I'd seen it since my arrival, and its current strong. I looked across to the other side as the Banoak house came into view. From this side, someone could watch the house and the people in it. I ran, the leaves crunching under my feet, drowning out all sounds except the river. I fanned away a dragonfly and moved a little closer to the river where a cleared path spread in front of me.

Without warning, my off-balanced, long skinny body landed in the roiling river. I had no chance to see who shoved me or to prepare for the river's velocity.

My Ruger disappeared in the swift flow. I had to concentrate on keeping my head up and getting my heavy shoes off. I felt for my ankle gun, but it had slipped out of the holster. Already fatigued from running, I zipped under Beatty's Bridge and downstream at a fast pace, trying to stay calm and flounder my way to the bank. No swimming in this muddy current.

Had Hawk been hiding out? Had he followed me and waited for an opportunity to get rid of me?

I saw tree limbs hanging out over the river, but I rushed past them before I could react. I soon saw more branches and grabbed at them but they broke off in my fingers. I'm not sure how far I went downstream before I saw the tree, bent far enough into the river for me to have a chance to grab something on it. I hit hard, managing to hang on to substantial tree growth by sheer determination.

If I didn't get to the bank fast, I'd be going on another water ride. I reached deep inside for the fortitude to throw my leg over, despite the pull of the river's current. Once on the tree, I shimmied to the bank and stretched out until I caught my breath and calmed down.

I sat up and studied the situation, watching a striped deck umbrella swirl by, only to fill up with water and sink. Several sizable river rocks came next, followed by a dog igloo, heading downstream at an alarming rate. Directly in front of me the river raged on. I turned my body. Behind me, a swamp full of slime-clad tree trunks and gross moss. It had a strong musty stench. I saw large pine trees at least a mile away. I'd have to tromp barefoot through swamp to find my way to any road.

I sighed and beat a few weeds as I started through the boggy mess, using cattails for leverage since my bare feet stuck in the mud as though it wanted to pull me under. I didn't like the feeling. Every move of my foot frightened me. I splashed and stomped to make as much noise as possible so that if any varmints lay in wait, maybe I'd scare them first.

Do alligators inhabit swamps this far inland? I knew snakes did. Large, nasty snakes.

I swatted some sort of bug about the size of a helicopter. He had already bitten me, and the evidence swelled on my arm. I crawled around a cypress knee, taking my time to look for snakes and other creepy things. Large snapping turtle heads peeked at me just above the water line.

Or are they large cottonmouths?

I reached a dam that seemed to cover most of the swamp where it narrowed near the pine trees. I pulled myself around it as an angry beaver went on the attack. I snatched my hand back just before he sunk his teeth in. I yelled, and he took a dive. I hoped he wouldn't take off my leg. I pulled myself up onto firm ground while two egrets perched in a nearby tree, watching the entertainment with beady eyes.

I wrestled the woods to find a highway. My watch had disappeared, but I knew it was late afternoon, and I was nowhere near the end of this ordeal. My feet were tender and laden with heavy mud and Heaven only knew what else, making my gait slow. I pushed on, determined to clear the woods before dark. I felt such relief when I found a road, but I had no idea where the road went. I headed in the direction I thought was north as an old truck sped past, slammed on the brakes, and backed up. I glanced over as the window rolled down. Cyrano Blood grinned through all the hair on his face.

"Why, Agent Hunter, what on earth are you doing? You look

like you've been in Hell Swamp, but I know you've got more sense than that. Jump in."

Having no energy to jump, I crawled in.

"I'd offer you a towel, but I'm just heading in from work and don't have one at the moment. What happened to you?"

I launched into my story, wondering if he had an alibi for the morning hours. I didn't mention my suspicions about Hawk Daw. When I'd finished, Mr. Blood had stopped smiling. I remained quiet the rest of the way while he filled me in on some stories from the swamp—pets and even a child missing over the years. I noticed a bottle of Nyquil on the dashboard, but didn't say anything about it.

He dropped me off at the Banoak house near my Hummer, a welcomed sight. I thanked him, hosed off behind the house, got into the Hummer once again, and headed to the beach, driving with bare scratched feet. I'd lost two guns, a watch, a pair of perfectly broken-in shoes, and a significant portion of my dignity. I'd gained gigantic whelps, bruises, and a new respect for Hell Swamp. If I were going to continue to be scratched up, I'd need some kind of antibacterial cream, and maybe even a tetanus shot. I worried about what I might have been exposed to in the river, and particularly in the muddy, bug, rodent, and reptile-infested swamp.

Seven

After retrieving more weapons from my Genesis Beach con-
do, scrubbing myself until I nearly bled, and getting a few hours
of shuteye, I rapped on Hawk Daw's door in the dawn fog. I intended to talk to him before he started his day and I couldn't find
him. Ethan opened the door.

"Hey, Agent Hunter. Boy, you're up early."

"Ethan, I need to talk with your father," I said, keeping a
professional demeanor.

"Sure." He turned and yelled, "Dad! Agent Hunter's here!" He
turned back to me. "I gotta get to school. See you, Agent Hunter,"
the tall young man said as he whisked by me with a book bag. I
watched as he climbed into the newer model truck and cranked
up, driving off with no licensed driver in the passenger seat beside him. I heard footsteps and turned back to see Hawk walking toward me. He looked embarrassed.

"Agent Hunter, back for breakfast?"

"No, Mr. Daw," I replied without breaking a smile. His smile
disappeared. "I have a few questions for you before you start
your day."

"Come on in and I'll fix you some coffee."

"No."

"Okay, then." He yanked his head back at my abruptness.

"Mr. Daw, we found a spotlight in Clara Banoak's bushes.
Right by the front door."

"A spotlight? What's that got to do with me?"

"Your fingerprints are on it."

His face reddened.

"My prints? Are you sure?"

"Yes sir. How do you explain that, Mr. Daw?"

"Well, I have several lights. Ethan and I use them for spotting deer during the off-season. And when we go camping or night fishing." He grunted. "I guess I should say when Ethan goes night fishing."

"You don't fish at night?"

"No. The only fishing I do is from the bank. I'm hydrophobic, and it's a long story. You don't seem in the mood to hear it."

"No, I'm not," I responded, although I was curious. "But back to the light. How do you account for a spotlight showing up at the murder scene with your prints on it?"

"Look, Agent Hunter, I don't like your tone. I've already told you I didn't kill Clara Banoak, and I honestly told you how I felt about her."

"I'm responsible for solving her murder. I don't care how you take my tone of voice. You have to realize you're now the prime suspect, Mr. Daw."

"Wait a minute! Wait just a damn minute!" He yelled and pulled at his hair while he paced inside his house. I stepped out on the porch, my fingers wrapped around my weapon. He joined me on the porch once he calmed down and put on some shoes.

"Listen, Agent Hunter, I swear to you, I did not kill that woman! I don't know how to explain my prints on that light. Look, can we just look at mine for a minute before you take me in?"

"I didn't say I was taking you in."

"You said I'm the main suspect, and you read me my Miranda rights when you came here the first time." His face twisted. "I can't believe this is happening!"

"I don't have enough evidence to take you in," I said.

"You mean *yet*."

"Is there more evidence, Mr. Daw?"

"Hell no! I didn't kill her." He stepped off the porch and stomped to his truck at a fast clip.

"Where are you going?" I yelled, running after him.

"I'm just making sure all my lights are here." He turned around as he opened the toolbox lid in the bed of his old farm truck. "Hey, you look, Agent Hunter. I don't want you to think I'm pulling a gun on you."

He backed away and put both hands on his head as I stepped to the toolbox with my hand on my weapon. He moved cautiously to a position where I could keep my eyes on him. I started taking crap out of the toolbox and placing it in the bed of the truck—a black spotlight with one million candlepower, a blaze orange light with three million candlepower, several orange hunting caps, some camo gloves, and a yellow and black spotlight with six million candlepower.

I looked up at him.

"Is this all?"

"No. Where's the white one?"

"There's not a white one in here." He walked over and looked for himself. Then he went through the truck's cab, even looking behind the seat. "Let's check the shed. We keep most of our hunting and camping gear in there."

I followed him to a small red out-building. The thirty-five minute search didn't reap a white light.

"Maybe that one's in the truck Ethan drove to school."

"Yeah, I noticed he drove by himself."

"Come on, Agent Hunter. Give me a break. He's fifteen and hates to ride the bus for an hour one-way. He's safe. Please don't make it an issue."

"Right now my concern is your fingerprint, Mr. Daw."

"We have two choices. We can get in your Hummer and drive twenty-five miles to the school, or I can call Ethan to look." He walked up to me. "Your choice."

"He has a cell phone?"

"Doesn't every kid?"

Hawk dialed Ethan and got him to put the teacher on, so he could tell her he needed his son to go to the truck to check something. The teacher agreed to let Ethan leave the classroom long enough to check. Ethan promised to call back.

The few minutes passed slowly, with plenty of distrust and anxiety passing between Hawk and me. When the cell phone rang, Hawk pressed the speaker button so I could hear the conversation.

"Dad? It's not in the truck, but I just remembered taking it on the camping trip with Huey a few weeks ago."

"You think you left it somewhere?"

"Maybe."

Hawk paused and looked at me. "Well, you need to speak with Agent Hunter. Hold on a second." He handed me the phone.

"Ethan?"

"Yes, ma'am?"

"What's up with the light?"

"I took it on a camping trip a couple of weeks ago. Me and my buddy, Huey, went cat fishing, and I always take a spotlight. I don't see it in the truck. I don't remember losing it, but it's possible."

"Okay, Ethan. What color was it?"

"The one I took camping was white, but we've got a bunch of different colors and powers."

"Okay. Thanks." I handed the phone to Hawk, who told his son not to worry, and that he loved him.

After he disconnected, he faced me, looking into my eyes.

"Agent Hunter, somebody found the light and used it in Clara Banoak's murder?"

"We think the killer used it to blind her and get the upper hand. Your print was very clear. No others."

"But I didn't kill her!"

"The killer probably wore gloves. I haven't found any other prints we can identify, even on the gambrel." Hawk looked washed out. "Look, I've got the information I came for. It sounds reasonable. Interrogations can be rough, but it's my job." I started to leave, then turned back.

"If you don't mind saying, why are you afraid of water?"

He cleared his throat and spoke in a softer, sadder voice than I had ever heard from him. "When I was a kid, about ten, there was a flash flood while some of us kids camped out with a few dads. My mother came to pick me up, and I stood not too far down the road, in a safe place, waiting for her." He stopped to take a breath. "The water kept coming up, and I would take a step or two back, you know, to stay out of it. Anyway, I saw her coming, and she got close enough so I could see her face. She hesitated for a second and then drove through the water on the road. It didn't seem too deep, but when she got about halfway, the water pushed the car right off the road and into a canal that dumps into the river. The last thing I saw was her face, terrified when she realized she was gone drown."

I couldn't speak. Part of me wanted to reach out and hug him, but I didn't move. He cleared his throat and turned his eyes away from me.

I took a step toward him. "I'm so sorry. That's something you never get over."

He nodded, then tugged my arm. "Agent Hunter, find this guy. I don't want anybody thinking I killed her. Like I said, I didn't like her, but I wouldn't kill a human being. Please believe me."

I wanted to.

If Ethan told the truth and accidentally left the light somewhere, anyone could have picked it up and used it in the murder.

Was somebody trying to frame Hawk?

I walked the river path where I'd been running the previous day, now wearing tight, uncomfortable black shoes, observing every movement and sound. I walked carefully, looking in all directions for any clue to who pushed me in. A swatch of cloth. A cigarette butt. Anything. I strapped on my new Glock and packed a new backup pistol in my ankle pocket, but I had no reason to use either on this fruitless trek, and by ten o'clock I returned to the Banoak house.

Nita's red Mustang convertible was in the driveway. She stepped out as I walked around to the side of the porch. "Good morning, Agent Hunter."

"Morning, Ms. Quicki." Dressed in tar black, wearing a rose-encircled hat with a thin veil that flopped over her long nose, and little makeup, her face looked ghostly.

"Have you made any progress?"

"Not much, I'm afraid."

"You don't look so good. Are you okay?"

"I'm fine." I didn't offer to tell her about my ordeal, my bruises, my scratches, and my trip down the river. But I wondered if she'd have an alibi if I asked her. She pulled out her long butt holder and placed the cancer stick in it, flicking fire from her cloisonné lighter. The first puff headed straight at me. I had to subdue my overwhelming desire to pistol-whip her.

"I thought of something since I saw you last, Agent Hunter. I guess you need to know this. Cyrano Blood threatened Mama a while back. I didn't witness it, but she told me he came to the house drunk, as usual, and told her if she didn't quit messing with him, she'd be sorry."

I glared at her. "Why didn't you think of that sooner, when we asked about enemies?"

"Well, she had so many. I mean, it could have been almost anybody who knew her." She twirled her necklace and then adjusted her watch.

"Did anybody witness this threat?"

"I don't think so. I just thought you might want to check it out. I'm not even sure it's true. Sometimes my mother exaggerated."

"You said 'drunk as usual'?" A long puff of smoke whisked away from me on a hot gust of breeze.

"Yeah. He often smells of whiskey or some kind of alcohol, even if he doesn't act drunk." She fidgeted with her hat and dress for a minute and walked toward the gravesite.

The graveside service for Clara Banoak began at eleven o'clock on the property by the river where her husband, Eli, rested. The day was sticky with late fall humidity, and the dark clouds drooping in the sky looked as though they'd burst at any moment. I didn't want to wear the heavy rain gear in the back of the Hummer, so I tucked a small black umbrella inside my thin jacket, just in case. I'd moved the Hummer down the road to give other people room in the driveways and around the yard, but I needn't have bothered. Few mourners attended.

I stood across from Nita in her floppy hat so I could be far enough away from that infernal smoke and still observe her actions and reactions. A murder victim's relatives were often considered prime suspects, particularly when violence played a part. But so far I'd uncovered no evidence to indicate she was anything more than a victim herself. Nonetheless, I didn't like her. She glanced at me, clearing her throat and still twisting the hell out of her necklace. I hoped I made her extremely uncomfortable.

A minister appeared from around some tall shrubbery near the old shed and stood opposite me. Someone introduced me to Rose Paul Hill, Clara's closest neighbor and possibly her only friend, and to Magnolia Rich, her part-time housekeeper. Acme Beavers and his family arrived next, followed by Woody Forbesch and Navel Face, who walked up just as the minister began.

"Brothers and sisters, it is with great sorrow that we come here today to mourn the death, the violent murder, of our dear sister Clara, a woman who fought for the rights of helpless animals everywhere. Clara went to great lengths to attempt to stop all hunting, not just here in Pender County but throughout the nation. She met with great opposition, for this, as you all know, is hunting country. And this country is full of hunters of every description.

"That fact didn't deter Clara Banoak. No, siree. She got legislation through to nearly put a halt to bear hunting in this county. She was able to get the limit and dates of the season shortened 'for the sake of God's creature, the bear.' She was influential in creating discourse about making it more difficult for our youth to hunt. She wanted the minimum age for an adult hunting license raised from sixteen to eighteen years of age. While she never got that passed due to her untimely death, others will champion her cause, I among them."

The minister, obviously an activist himself, didn't mind using Clara's funeral to promote his own agenda. I supposed Clara would be proud. And I thought it interesting that no other animal-rights activists came to her graveside service. Perhaps the dignitaries she wined and dined didn't want their names even mentioned in connection with this act of violence.

"Clara Banoak, misunderstood by many, died a violent death just because her views differed from others around her. I'm certain that God has a special place in Heaven reserved for her, where animals graze unfettered, as all God's creatures should."

The minister said a short prayer, and Nita threw a handful of dirt on the casket after it descended into the ground. Then a small load of gravel poured out on top of it because of the grave's close proximity to the river and underground springs. The gravel would keep the casket from rising if the river flooded.

We walked away, leaving the victim's daughter to stand by herself. I glanced at Acme, who had shown up in spite of being a hunter. I could imagine him seething from the minister's words. And I couldn't help but notice that he planted himself near Nita rather than his wife and family. A few people whispered to each other, and then went to their trucks and left.

The weathered house still had Christmas lights up from last year. Not the tiny white lacy-looking kind, but the big old-fashioned bulbs in all colors, waiting to be switched on again soon. I tapped on the door as a lazy overweight bulldog ambled up to sniff me. I stuck out my fist; he sniffed and curled up on a tuft of dead grass. I guess he figured I wasn't worth biting. I knocked louder. Even though an old car sat in the driveway, apparently she wasn't home, this woman, Rose Hill, who'd left a message she wanted to talk to me. Her house was across the road and about one hundred yards east of Clara Banoak's house. Neighbors. She'd been at the funeral. Perhaps she'd seen or heard something of value to this case. I wouldn't find out today though. I patted the dog's head and left.

I stood up and watched Cyrano Blood as he pulled his truck up to the house.

"Agent Hunter, what a nice surprise!"

"I hope you don't mind my sitting out here on the deck waiting for you."

"Not at all. In fact, I'm fixing to fry up some fresh catfish. Ever had them?"

"No, I don't think so." I stood up. "Look Mr. Blood..."

"Cy." He grinned like a mule eating briars. Behind all the wild hair gentle eyes glistened—bloodshot, but gentle.

"Mr. Blood, we need to talk. I've got some allegations."

"Against me, no doubt."

I nodded.

"Look, Agent Hunter, I look rough. Wild even. But I'm not a murderer. Go ahead. Spit it out. What're the allegations this time?"

"Clara Banoak told her daughter you threatened her a while back. Is that true?"

He scratched his head full of white scruffy hair with obvious irritation.

"Sir?"

"Dang nabbit! That's been years ago. Why is it coming up now?" He looked at me sternly. "I guess I did threaten her. A long time ago. But she'd threatened me too. The day in question, a Saturday. I'd docked my fishing boat at her raggedy dock because mine disintegrated and I hadn't had time to fix it. She came up here and cussed and carried on like a maniac. I told her I'd move it, that I hadn't intentionally meant to upset her, and I apologized then. I told her I should have gotten her permission before I did it. The dock was about rotten, so I don't know what the problem was. She never used the damn thing!

"Anyway, when I went to get the boat on Sunday, it had sunk, and I don't mean by itself. Big gashes in it, like from an axe. I admit I stomped up to her door and told her off. I may have said a few things I shouldn't have, but I'd already told her I'd get it. No reason for her to destroy it. She was just mean that way."

"How long ago did this happen?"

"It's been two or three years. Maybe more. I don't know why Nita would even bring it up now. I just want all of 'em to leave me the hell alone! I'm not a bad person, Agent Hunter. Faults? Yeah, I got plenty. But I didn't kill Clara Banoak."

As I stared at him, trying to figure him out, he managed to smile. "Now rest a spell while I cook these fish."

"I have to go."

"Why are you so skiddish? Are you afraid of me, Agent Hunter?"

"No, I'm not."

His face softened. "Then let me treat you to a nice supper. I promise not to poison you. In fact, since you want to be obstinate, you can grate the cabbage." His face broke into a grin, not a smart-ass grin but a kind, well meaning grin. At least, that's the way I read it. Or maybe my hunger coaxed me to stay.

He opened the door, and I hesitantly stepped into his house. I liked the den. The white walls had plenty of old weathered beams and a wide wood plank floor to warm them. His granite hearth stood tall and deep enough to cook a pot of deer stew. Three iron pitchfork tines leaned against the wall above the mantle. I'd seen them earlier when I peeked in a window. A wooden washtub on the floor displayed kindling and lightwood knots. The sparse furniture looked masculine in brown leather, but beautifully embroidered accent pillows softened the look.

A wood saddle stand behind the sofa held two leather saddles. When I asked why he kept them inside, he said, "To keep the horses from chewing them up."

I smiled.

A narrow bookcase in the corner was home to an extensive collection of novels, mostly the classics, and other shelves were filled with Reader's Digest Condensed Book volumes, and recent novels by Sandford, Patterson, Deaver, and North Carolina's Maron, Hart and Lane. A group of cross-stitched samplers above the bookcase seemed out of place with the rustic setting and intense novels. I examined them.

"I stitched those, you know," he called out, still grinning.

"No way!"

"Yep, my wife, bless her heart and rest her soul, taught me to cross-stitch while we stayed shut in together for long days and nights. She had unbelievable patience. The two samplers on the far right are hers; the others are mine. I have more of her work in the bedrooms, and those pillows on the sofa are ones I did. Nobody believes a big burly man like me does needlework though. It calms me. It's very relaxing on a winter's night. I don't enjoy television as much as most men, I suppose. I'd rather be doing something constructive."

"What happened to your wife?"

"Cancer. Malicious stuff. I took a leave of absence from work to stay home with her. It didn't take long. She was pretty much covered with it by the time she went to the doctor. Three months later in the spring, I buried her. At least, we had one last Christmas together."

"How long ago?"

"Seven years. It doesn't seem like it," he said, sounding wistful.

"I know you miss her."

His eyes watered and his face showed his pain.

I kept both eyes on him and both guns nearby, although my suspicious feelings softened a bit. We got through a delicious supper without a problem. The fresh catfish and slaw were great with his potatoes, loaded with cheese, butter, and fresh chives from his own herb garden on the porch. I enjoyed his humor and hoped a conniving killer wasn't drawing me in. Intuition told me he was safe, and I always trusted my gut. I thanked him for the meal and prepared to leave.

"I need to ask you a question."

"Anything."

"Where were you the night Clara Banoak died?"

"We had the big county Relay for Life banquet for all cancer survivors that night. Pender County and Onslow County joined efforts. I was in Burgaw from five in the afternoon until after midnight. I'm on the serving committee, which means setting up, cooking and serving, and cleaning up afterwards."

"Can anyone verify your presence there the whole time?"

"Plenty of people. I'll make you a list." He jotted about ten names on a piece of yellow memo paper, tore it off, and handed it to me. I thanked him.

"Watch out for yourself, Agent Hunter. And be careful what you believe. There are many liars around here."

Eight

The next day Cyrano Blood talked me into riding around and looking at the river. This time we took a vehicle rather than horses. He said he had a theory about how the murderer got to Clara without being seen. Curiosity won out.

"I fried us some chicken and brought along some fresh yeast rolls. Hope that's enough."

"You shouldn't have, but I'm glad you did. I can't remember the last time I had a piece of good fried chicken or a yeast roll."

He grinned. "If you eat enough stale mess from Yonder Store, you'll figure some way to get something better. I like to cook, and usually pick up groceries coming in from work. I don't eat out much—not that there's anywhere around here to eat anyway."

"Did you bake the rolls yourself?"

"You betcha."

"You could always open your own place."

"No thanks. Besides, people think I'm strange, so they probably wouldn't eat my food." He smiled. "You know you're taking a risk, don't you?"

"Yeah, but the catfish didn't kill me, so I figure I'll try some more of that good cooking," I answered, winking at him.

He laughed aloud as we turned into a path that led to the river. We left civilization far behind.

Miss Smarty Britches, what in the hell are you doing out here in the middle of nowhere with this man? He could cut your head off and bury you in river mulch where you'd never be found!

I didn't know why I'd come. Wait. Yes, I did. Curiosity. The same kind that kills cats. I instinctively liked Cyrano Blood, but as I glanced at the Nyquil bottle on his dashboard again, I had second thoughts. I trusted my intuition but shivered just the same.

Once we parked, I followed him toward some foliage. I inhaled the unmistakable fragrance of bald cypress trees wading along the river's edge.

"Aha!" he grinned, holding up a tiny plant in his hand. "It's just about impossible to find herbs this late in the year, but here they are!" His big hand held a plant with its roots still intact. "Angelica."

His delight over the little plants amused me. "O...kay, and what do you do with that?"

"It's sweet. I add a little to desserts like cobblers and pies."

I nodded, trying to hide my growing impatience. I followed him while he brushed back mulch in some moist, shady areas not too far from the riverbank and plucked the little plants. "Have you ever seen Cicely?"

I shook my head, showing my ignorance of herbs.

He held up another kind of plant. "This here is good when you run out of sugar and the store is thirty miles away. It's another good substitute."

"Mr. Blood, I really don't have time to hunt herbs. I've got this case to solve. You know, a murder case?"

He turned and looked at me, moving his big hand slightly. "Call me Cy, now. I insist. Be patient with me, Agent Hunter."

Cyrano Blood was a thick man. Not thick in the head; no, he was intelligent, but he had a thick build. His wild white hair just made him appear to be...what? Dangerous? I gulped as he continued on, studying the ground for a while before crossing a low place in the river where rocks beckoned. I stood in the middle of the river balanced on two stones, wondering how the water level dropped so quickly.

Cy looked back at me and grinned through his wiry mustache. "Beautiful, isn't it?"

The trees I saw down the river on the western bank looked as though they were ablaze, the first sun of the day seeping through the fall foliage. Even the water itself seemed to be on fire, with only slight movement. I clicked the imaginary camera in my brain, wanting to hold on to the beauty even while we searched for traces of hostility all around it.

"Down that way is a stand of bald cypress trees estimated to be over seventeen hundred years old. I'd take you, but it's quite difficult to get to them."

"I'll take your word for it."

"Look at this, Agent Hunter. It looks like a boat pulled up in here." I walked over to where he stood beside it, only half-interested.

"But isn't that common?"

"Not really. Most boats put in at the ramp about a half-mile farther down. It seems odd to bring a boat to the bank right in front of Clara Banoak's house."

He had my attention. I looked up and saw the house through some trees. I checked the boat over, but no name or number on it could identify its owner. I remembered the cam in my pocket and took a few pictures.

"We may need to search even closer. This is about where I got shoved into the river, but I don't remember seeing a boat here at the time."

"Did you ever find out who pushed you in?"

"Not yet."

"My guess is somebody thinks you're getting too close, or they just don't like snoopers."

Cyrano walked on and pulled the leaves off a plant.

"What's that one?"

"Woodruff. Put some of this in between your linens and they'll smell great even if they stay on the closet shelf a while." I needed to take notes. "I make some sachets every year for the church bazaar. One year I made some to sell for a little two-year-old kid who had leukemia. We raised several hundred dollars and it didn't cost me anything but some cheap material and thread."

Nobody had told me what a big heart Cyrano had, only that he was strange. Different, in my opinion, wasn't necessarily a bad thing. This man was unique and talented.

"Come look at this, Agent Hunter." He stood between the river and a large tree. As I walked over he pointed to a brass stake embedded in it.

"What's that for?"

"That, young lady, is where the ferry or riverboat tied up. Probably well over one-hundred years ago."

"Really? Tell me more," I said, meeting his gentle eyes.

"Well, long before your parents were even a thought, there were no bridges across the Black River. I'm talking the late 1800's now. Before we had all them fancy engineers to design answers to transportation problems." He sat down on a cypress stump and pulled up some rabbit tobacco to suck on. I crouched near him as he continued the history lesson.

"Anyway, ferries and riverboats up and down the river got folks from one place to another." He looked straight at me for a second. "We take all of our conveniences for granted, don't we?"

I nodded.

"If you know anyone around here with a decent boat, you might want to drift from here to Mill Creek. You'd see some interesting sights to be sure."

"Like what?"

"Swamps you didn't know existed—bigger and uglier than Hell Swamp, with an odor you'd never forget. And snakes of every kind. In one place the river's so narrow, water ash and cat-briar from both sides of the river create a canopy all the way over the water."

"I bet the snakes love it," I added with a case of the heebie-jeebies.

"You betcha. The biggest rattler I've ever seen was down there. As big around as my arm." And his arm was big.

Cyrano and I both stood up.

"I guess I've bored you enough. Let's go."

"I've enjoyed the lessons."

On our way back to the truck, he bent over, looking closely at the ground.

"What herb have you found this time, Cy?"

He stood erect and kicked at the ground with a concerned look on his face. "These aren't herbs. It looks like a pet cemetery. Or, most likely, where they were tortured."

"What?" I walked over and peered at the charred remains of what appeared to be cats and small dogs. Cy moved around the area while I stood motionless, not sure what to do.

"There's been a campfire here. I don't like the looks of this," he said. "Stay here. I'll get my shovel from the truck. And then, Agent Hunter, I want you to investigate this." His hefty form shaded me. "Do you hear me?"

I dipped my head in silence and took pictures while I waited for him. He came back and buried the remains without either of us saying a word.

"Something evil this way comes, Agent Hunter."

"Are you saying that because of the animals?"

"Yep. And I've been hearing some of the kids around here are snatching cats. Dogs too, evidently."

"Why?"

"Rumor has it there's a little group of Satan-worshippers at the high school. I never took much stock in rumors. I never thought much about it being true. Until this. This looks bad."

I had to agree.

"Have you heard any names?"

"No." He looked up into the trees, not making eye contact. If he knew anything, he wasn't saying. I didn't ask if Lilith Huff-stickle's name had come up.

As we walked around the animal gravesite, I maneuvered around a bush, watching where I stepped.

"Whoa!" I slammed on brakes.

Cy stopped.

"What is it?"

"It looks like a body. A head. Someone's head," I said, crouching under the bush for a better look. I stood up just as Cy leaned over my shoulder and nearly knocked him to the ground. He got in front of me and poked at the baldhead with a twig.

"No, let me do it, Cy. The area might have to be cordoned off."

While he lifted the bush's thin limbs, I brushed the dirt and leaves gently, gradually revealing an entire face. A face where the flesh under each eye had been pulled all the way to the lips and pierced to the top lip with a steel hoop. A face with piercings in both nostrils. A face with a mouthful of oversized teeth, the jaws having been cut and pierced all the way to the ears, the chin pierced with another hoop ring. With my fingers, I gently moved the debris surrounding it. With relief, I recognized thick rubber, and raked out the mask with a glove I'd found in my pocket.

"Probably left over from Halloween a few weeks back," Cy said.

I lifted the mask on my twig and noticed a three-barbed ring tattoo on the baldhead.

Did it mean anything? Could the mask be connected to anything other than the animals?

I'm taking this in just in case it connects to something significant."

"Let's head back now. We've got some chicken to eat."

I had been hungry a minute ago, but my appetite waned considerably with the discovery of dead pets and the initial scare of the mask. It looked so real I found myself trembling. I started toward Cy and noticed a swatch of material on the ground. I knelt to pick up the piece of black fabric like the scrap I'd found in the Banoak yard.

Had someone stolen pets and brought them here to torture?

Nine

I promised to have Thanksgiving dinner with Mama, glad her assisted-living facility was about an hour from this crime scene and not six hours across the state. She was excited that I could come, and I'd been to visit enough on holidays to know there would be a feast in the formal dining room with linen tablecloths and napkins for all the residents who could sit at tables. I wheeled into the Krispy Kreme drive-thru to get her a box of glazed doughnuts for later. She would love them.

I went to Mama's studio apartment and peeked in. She dozed in her favorite chair by the window, the sunshine, no doubt, warming and comforting her. I smiled and stepped in as quietly as I could. Her head popped up.

"Logan! You're early! I'm so glad you came. I've told everybody you'd sit with me at dinner."

I kissed her cheek, put down the pastries, and sat on her single bed, taking her hands in mine.

"You look wonderful, Mama." She really didn't, but she made a strong effort to cover the fact that she was ill. "Purple is definitely your color." Her shirt and pants matched. Around her neck she'd slipped a gorgeous necklace with some of the same color in it.

"I wanted to look special for Thanksgiving. Some of the ladies will have on turkey sweaters, but I'm not wearing a turkey on my breasts."

I snickered. She didn't. I rubbed her hands, so swollen with arthritis and fluid. I glanced at her feet, running over the tops of her shoes and almost beyond recognition. She had to be in pain. It was amazing she could walk on them.

"Can you tell a difference since your pacemaker was installed?"

"Not really. The doctor said it would help my circulation and that, in turn, would get rid of some of this fluid, but it hasn't helped a bit that I can tell. All I do is pee."

"I believe he also said some exercise would help."

"Logan, you know I'm in no shape to exercise. I can barely manage to walk to the elevator and get downstairs to the dining room. I have to use the walker all the time now." She pointed to several different types in the corner. "Get it, and let's go on down. There'll be a crowd today. It's a buffet, so you'll have to fix me a plate. I can't stand in line." I put the quad walking stick in front of her. "No. I need the one with four legs."

"Have you fallen?"

"No, and I don't plan to again. But I wobble sometimes."

"Again? When did you fall, Mama?"

"Oh, shoot! I wasn't gone tell you that."

"Out with it! Somebody should have called me!"

"I fell flat on my face and broke my nose. I couldn't get my hands out fast enough to stop myself. Those new sandals I thought I had to buy tripped me up. I gave them to the housekeeper."

I sighed. "Mama, why didn't you call me?"

"Nothing you could do. The folks here picked me up and took me to the ER in their van. Even the doctors said they couldn't do anything about it. They just washed the blood off and sent me back here. I'm sure I'll pay dearly for that trip. I haven't got the bill yet."

I could feel the blood rising in my throat from anger, or maybe worry. The woman I had known all my life, who'd been fiercely independent and confident, was leaving me behind in a hurry.

New sandals? More likely loss of balance from feet about to explode.

"Well, are you coming, Logan?"

I ran to open the door for her, noting that she still had a healthy dose of impatience.

We enjoyed our turkey, dressing, and cranberry relish, but Mama refused to eat the broccoli. I found her a small salad instead, but lettuce and little else didn't suit her either. She said she didn't usually stay for dessert, but when I told her she could choose from coconut, sweet potato, or chocolate pie, she chose coconut, and I chose chocolate. I scooted closer to her, and we shared both, savoring the sweets and our precious time together. I had to wonder how much more time I had with her, a woman old before her time, a defective heart robbing her of many productive years.

Late that afternoon, on my way back to Black River, I noticed many yards filled with cars and trucks, children running around and playing in leaves, recently raked into high piles, and families and friends hugging and laughing. Thanksgiving Day. A day to count our many blessings and be with those we love. I enjoyed my visit with Mama. It had been pleasant from start to finish. She didn't beg me to stay. She didn't complain about my job or not calling often enough, although I called every Saturday morning at nine o'clock sharp, and she could take that to the bank.

Some folks busied themselves setting up yard decorations for Christmas. Even Mr. Gaddy went all out. Colored lights attached to some kind of netting ran back and forth on his roof. I looked in my rearview mirror, and with no cars behind me, I stopped in the middle of the road and giggled until I broke out in a full-blown howl. A partially inflated and extremely jolly Santa in front of the house waved at me. He appeared to be humping Rudolph, well inflated and right in front of him.

Next to this rowdy Santa, Frosty and his family wobbled in a huge snow globe. At this point in the inflation process, Frosty's carrot nose seemed to be firmly wedged into Mrs. Frosty's large white buttocks. He grinned to the brim of his black top hat. I eased on down the road as Mr. Gaddy and some children strung twinkling colored lights on his antique John Deere tractor near the road and plugged them in with an orange heavy-duty extension cord. He barely moved but still enjoyed the children's laughter and the holiday spirit.

Hawk Daw had more tasteful decorations. White icicle lights hung from the roof, and I could see a tree with clear lights through the front window. Sly Foxx decorated a tree in the yard with large red bulbs. I blew the horn as I drove by and he waved back. His front door held a plush green wreath adorned with a red bow. A few miles farther down, Yonder Store blinked lights all over the front, some white, some colored. All tacky.

I turned into the driveway of Clara's neighbor, Rose Hill. She now had her Christmas lights turned on, about every third one burned out across the entire front of the house's roof. She answered my first knock.

"Logan Hunter, ma'am. SBI."

"I remember you."

She opened the door, and I stepped inside as a surprising whiff of spiced cider curled through my nostrils.

She's starting early, isn't she?

The living room had a wall-to-wall mantle, loaded with pictures, pottery, and books with a large old hearth in its center. Three beautiful antique plates hung down off the front of the mantle. White shelves took up the rest of the space on either side of the hearth. The shelves on the right side had glass doors from behind which an array of magazines peeked. I recognized the gold color of *The National Geographic*. The other side of the hearth was open shelves filled with pottery and ceramics.

An old oak trunk served as a coffee table in front of the fireplace, where two pots of Lamb's Ear drooped over a basket of picture postcards. Two antiquated rose-colored chairs sat near the trunk, their velvet nearly rubbed off.

Rose Hill motioned me to one while she took the other. "It sure has taken you a long time to get here," she said, her voice raspy. Her false teeth, that obviously didn't fit her mouth, clacked as she spoke. The clacking instantly annoyed me.

"I came as soon as I got the message, but you weren't home that day. Or, at least, no one came to the door."

"Hmmm. I don't know where I could have been. My name is Rose Paul Hill," she clacked. I nodded. "Clara and I go back a long ways."

"Yes, I remember you from the funeral. Do you have some specific information, Ms. Hill?" I stroked the lace fabric under an antique vase, waiting for her response.

Clack. "Call me Rose Paul. Would you care for some cider?"

"No thanks, but it smells wonderful."

"And that's why I keep some on the stove from Thanksgiving until after New Year's. I don't really drink it much, but the house sure does smell good."

I looked around at her appealing room.

"I see you like fine things too, Agent Hunter." Clack. "I'm a collector. All the things I cherish are around me. Lace, silk scarves, linen tablecloths, you name it. I use them. It doesn't make any sense to store the things you love. They dry rot." Clack. "I figure there's not another person alive who'd feel the same as I do about my stuff. Since I don't have children, most of it would end up in a yard sale, I imagine, so I'm enjoying it all now."

"That sounds like a good philosophy to have."

"I'm sure you know by now that Clara had enemies, Agent Hunter. I got along with her fine, but I stayed out of her political affairs. She never used her fine linens or her fine china except when bigwigs showed up to meet with her, at her insistence, I think.

"Yes, she just kept it packed up most of the time and used paper products instead, even for her close friends and even at Christmas, I'm told. I reckon her daughter, Nita, will get it all, although, I can't say much for her. Married Lord only knows how many times, and none of them lasted. She's always out gallivanting around." Clack.

A silence grew as she stared at nothing I could identify.

"Is there anything specific you'd like to tell me? Did you see anybody there the day she was killed? Did you hear anything?"

Clack. "I think they said she was killed at night. I didn't see anything, but I heard some commotion coming from the river." Clack.

"What kind of commotion?"

"Like a bunch of fishermen in boats. You know, some of them still have fish fries on the bank once in a while, especially when the herrings run." Clack.

"Could that have been going on?"

"No. The herrings run in the spring." Clack. She blinked at me as though I knew that.

"Rose Paul, we've covered every inch of the bank. And yes, we think she was killed after dark, but we didn't find much of anything that relates to the case. Did you recognize any voices?"

"No. What noise I heard I figured was men fishing, and maybe camping out on a sand bar. It never occurred to me something else was going on." Clack. "Clara could always take care of herself anyway. She knew how to shoot a shotgun."

I thanked her and headed toward the door.

"Oh, Agent Hunter, you might want to speak to Richard though."

"Who?"

"Richard Leak. Everybody calls him Dick, but I think that's terrible." Clack. "Anyhow, he's kind of a know-it-all, if you can get the straight of what he's telling you."

"How's that?"

"He's deaf as a bed post, or at least, he plays it that way. He always seems to know everything about everybody. Some people say they've seen him behind trees and in shrubs minding everybody's business but his own. You can usually find him at Yonder Store or over in Atkinson, somewhere there's people and a chair to sit in. He drives an old white Cadillac." Clack. "One of those big gas-guzzlers. He ought to be ashamed of wasting gas with it costing so blooming much now."

I made a note about Mr. Leak.

Then I parked beside Nita Quicki's convertible in the Banoak backyard and found her digging a hole with a shovel.

She pointed to a picnic basket sitting beside a bench on the patio between the back of the house and the river. "Agent Hunter, I brought you some dinner."

She dropped her shovel, grabbed a blanket sitting next to the basket, and spread it out. As I stood by, somewhat stunned by this gesture, she lifted a bottle of Black River Red and two flutes out of the basket, along with cheese, bread, fruit, and a container of unknown spread.

"What are you doing with the shovel?"

She sighed and plopped down on the large blanket. I walked over and stood over her. "I hope you like chicken salad. Who would believe we could have a picnic the last week in November? The weather's so strange." She pulled her blue sweater around her, and I curled my longs legs under me and sat on the other side of the blanket. She popped the cork on the tall bottle of Duplin wine and poured it into my flute as I sneezed.

"Bless you!"

"Thanks. There's still something in the air that triggers my allergies." She nodded while I took a good look at the wine. "You have great taste in wine. This is one of many Duplin Winery favorites of mine. And since we're sitting here by Black River, it's perfect. But, back to my question, Ms. Quicki."

"Is there a problem with digging in my own yard, Agent Hunter?" Her tone didn't fit a picnic. She guzzled her wine.

"I don't suppose so. I was just curious." I looked at her over the edge of my flute and took a sip.

"I know you're still investigating Mama's murder and all, but the crime tape is gone, and, well, I did ask Sheriff Gunn before I started."

"Okay," I said, still curious, but not asking again.

We ate fresh chicken salad sandwiches with hoop cheese and

crispy seedless grapes, accompanied by occasional bouts of small talk. The food, good and refreshing, filled the uncomfortable silence between us. We emptied the wine bottle and most of the salad container. I could have eaten the whole loaf of homemade bread by myself but used restraint.

When she finished her last bite, Nita stood.

"I'll answer your question, Agent Hunter. I'm sure you'll hear anyway. My mother left a will, and, of course, she left everything to me since I'm an only child. Daddy hoarded money, although he left Mama and me plenty. However, there's four-hundred twenty-three dollars and seventy-two fricking cents in the bank. Mr. Barnhill, the banker, said Daddy never had any faith in banks, so he seldom deposited anything. He figures he buried it somewhere on the grounds."

I stood up as I took in that bit of information. "You're kidding! I didn't know people did that anymore."

"I didn't either. Mama always seemed to have plenty of cash when I needed it though, so I figure it's around here somewhere. Look," she said, gathering her blanket, "I'm digging up the whole damn yard if I have to. It infuriates me that she put me in this position. What a bitch!" She spat the words out.

I stared at her for a second. "I can't stop you. But you might want to remember that the more folks who know about this, the more likely they will come to look for it themselves."

"I haven't told anybody but you and the sheriff, and I trust you'll be discreet." She started to head back to her shovel, but stopped and turned around. "Agent Hunter, I'm sorry to be so brusque. I'm not as hateful as I sound."

Yeah, right.

"I'm just upset about the money and the murder of my mother. Have you found out anything new about the case? Do you have any strong suspects? I, well, you know. She was my mother even if she was a lunatic."

"I can't say I've made much progress, Ms. Quicki. As you know, so many people got into the house and tracked through the scene before I got here. It rained that same afternoon, wiping out any tracks outside. It's a slow process. We tried to get prints from the gambrel and rope, but no luck. I assure you I'll call if I find out anything you need to know."

I watched her walk across the yard with her nose in the air and her backside swinging a little too much to be natural. My dislike for her deepened. I never felt very comfortable around her. And the picnic made me even more suspicious of her motives. Nita Quicki was an untrustworthy manipulator, so I made certain she drank and ate the food before I touched mine. I wasn't brainless.

Ten

I hadn't talked with Woody Forbesch yet, so I pulled into the paved lot in front of his paint and hardware store. Three pickups out front, one with a deerhound in the back, and one old white Cadillac that took up two spaces. I walked inside and meandered through the aisles while I waited for him to finish with his customers. I had to adjust my eyes from the bright sun to the dark store anyway.

I saw an array of quality interior and exterior paints, nails, nuts, bolts, screws—the typical stuff. But Mr. Forbesch also had a section in the back that included all kinds of gun shells, bullets, black powder, hunting knives, gutting knives, and two gambrels, along with a small selection of camo clothing and orange caps.

Two old gentlemen sat near a potbellied stove. Mr. Forbesch stood at the cash register, giving change to another one. He nodded at the two men and they put out their pipes.

"Excuse me, Mr. Forbesch?"

"Hey! Yes, ma'am. How are you?"

"I'm fine, thanks. Look, I need to talk to you, sir, but does that Cadillac outside belong to Mr. Richard Leak?"

"Yes. I don't see him right this minute though. He may be in the crapper. Oh, I mean, the bathroom."

I smiled and nodded. I intended to talk to Mr. Leak before I left.

The store owner approached and threw out his hand. I shook it.

"Agent Hunter, could I possibly do anything for you?"

"Yes, Mr. Forbesch, I need to ask some questions."

"Now, what did I tell you about that? It's Coon." He smiled through his black goatee, grown since I'd first met him.

"Yes, I remember. You have quite a selection of things in your store."

"I do. Yonder Store used to sell hardware, and I sold primarily paint, but the owner started adding more groceries because it's so far to the nearest real grocery store. He asked me to take his hardware inventory so he'd have more room for things like milk, bread, that sorta thing."

"I guess that was good for both of you, but there doesn't seem to be much in the line of groceries over there."

"It's worked out right well, although Mr. Jessup retired and moved to Florida. The current owner is really a farmer and doesn't do much at all with the store. I think he has trouble with supply trucks coming when he's in the field and can't open up. That's the reason so much of his stuff is out of date. Anyway, I keep inventory the hunters like since Wilmington is about forty miles away. Right now I only have a few clothes for boys."

"I notice you have gambrels."

"Yes, ma'am, and deer stands too. I don't know how much you know about hunting, Agent Hunter, but after each season, they build more stands and get them up for the next season. That way the deer get used to having the stand out there, and sometimes go right up to it even during hunting season."

"Do you sell many of those knives?" I pointed to several in a locked display case.

"Yep, and bows and arrows too. Every hunter's got 'em, and I sold two knives this week. Young boys just learning to shoot. Part of the deal with most of the fathers, is 'you kill it, you gut it'."

"That would be a good reason not to ever hunt as far as I'm concerned."

He laughed.

"I probably don't have much that would interest a lady like

yourself unless you garden. I have a nice inventory of shovels, rakes, and pitchforks."

I shook my head.

He motioned me to the empty rockers by the stove and handed me a refreshing orange cream drink. I didn't know they still made them.

"It's on the house."

"Thanks."

"Mr....um, Coon, I'm sure you know why I've come. I need to ask you the same questions I'm asking everyone else."

"Go right ahead. I probably won't have another customer until after school gets out unless somebody gets lost and needs directions."

I turned toward the front window and realized that while I'd been talking to him in the back of the store, the old Cadillac had left the premises.

"Where's the Cadillac that was parked there?"

"That old rattletrap is Dick Leak's. He comes around about every day or so. He musta left while we were walking around."

Crap!

"I needed to speak to him."

"You just missed him, I reckon, but like I said, he'll be around. Probably tomorrow."

"I'll have to catch up with him then, I suppose."

"He's pretty easy to find. Usually got his nose stuck in somebody else's business."

"There seems to be an epidemic of that around here."

"You got that right."

"Well then, back to the questions I came here to ask you. Clara Banoak. How do you know her?"

"I haven't lived here as long as most of these folks. I'm a transplant from upstate New York. Don't sound like it, do I?"

I shook my head. "Not at all."

"My dad used to come down to North Carolina to hunt with an old Army buddy of his. He fell in love with a piece of land between here and Atkinson. He bought nine hundred acres, posted it, and fenced it all in so he could bring some of his New York friends down to hunt. He built a house and some out buildings, and put up a gate to keep the hunters here from going on the land and killing everything when he went back to New York.

"He died some years back and left it to me, so now that's where I live. Anyway, he never mentioned having trouble with a woman down here, but since he died, I've been told Clara Banoak gave him a fit every time he came and brought a bunch of men. She couldn't get on his land, but if she saw him around, she'd have something sharp to say.

"My daddy would shoot words right back. The older hunters said he gave as good as he got. She'd always end up madder than a beaver in a plastic factory after it was all over."

"Did you ever meet her?"

"Not formally, although I knew who she was. She was a nasty little woman. She couldn't have had any friends. Even her facial expression was as sour as unsweetened prune juice." He turned red. "I do know her daughter, Nita, though."

"How well?"

"Well, it's like this, Agent Hunter. She comes in here about once a week, trying to rope me into a relationship, but I've heard too much about her. Damn if that woman don't have extra loose britches—if you know what I mean."

I did. And I didn't want to go there.

"Do you hunt?"

"Not much. I bird hunt now and again, but I stay busy trying to keep the rest of them going. It never appealed to me that much, and besides, the birds are about gone."

"Why is that?"

"We have a lot of foxes around here now, and a few coyotes. They eat the quail. There's a lot of red-tailed hawks around too."

"Oh," I said, handing him my empty drink bottle. "So you didn't have a personal beef with Ms. Banoak?"

"No."

"Coon, I need a list of people you've sold gutting knives and gambrels to. Can you do that for me?"

He scratched his balding head. "Whew! That's gone be tough. I sell 'em, but I don't write down names unless it's a gun. And I don't sell guns anymore 'cause I'd get robbed every weekend. I only sell gun shells. I got every kind of shell you can think of in here."

"Can you remember the last few you sold? I'm grasping at straws here. I need a break in this case."

"I know it must be tough. Most of the folks around here aren't gonna open up to a stranger—that being you."

That I already knew.

Coon walked me out to the Hummer. When I opened the door to get in, I saw my front tire. Flat as road kill.

"Damn it!"

"Oh, my. I'll get it, Agent Hunter. You got a spare?"

"Yeah, I think so."

"You must have caught a nail just right." He jacked up the front and pulled off the flat tire before getting the spare on. Once he tightened the lug nuts, he examined the flat, looking up into my eyes.

"Agent Hunter, this wasn't done by a nail. It was stabbed with a knife several times. See these slits?"

I bent down to look.

"You better watch your back."

Eleven

I heard her blaring, whiney voice before I got to the door of the house built of river stones. Whiney gossiped with some women about another poor woman who apparently wasn't there to defend herself. I knocked, and the conversation inside instantly ceased. The door snatched open, and I displayed my badge to the woman whose frayed long orange hair looked like it belonged on a scarecrow, her face not much better. Her body resembled a julienned carrot stick.

"SBI. I'm here to speak to a Ms. Magnolia Rich."

"Oh," the whiney voice said. "MAGNOLIA?" I flinched.

How can such a tiny stick of a woman be so loud and obnoxious?

A petite black woman came from behind the group. She looked frightened. "Now, Magnolia, if you've done something illegal, I'll have to let you go."

"She hasn't," I responded with an intentional scowl, really wanting to punch this broad. I asked Ms. Rich to step outside with me, away from the nosy, snotty women. We walked a few yards down the dirt driveway and stopped.

"Ms. Rich, I understand you kept house for Clara Banoak."

She nodded with her head tilted down and eyes diverted. "Yes'm."

"Tell me about the house and Ms. Banoak. Did she have many friends? Did she entertain often? Do you know of any enemies?"

"She usta have pahties. Invite fancy folk, you know, like congressmens and senatahs. She political. I works my behind off gettin' the house and the food ready for 'em. I cooks collard greens and yams, and she want big roasted turkey and ham and roast beef.

"She put on the dog when them fancy folk around. She get all dolled up with a fancy frock and too much color in her cheeks. And her lips too red. But Miss Clara stop havin' pahties when Mr. Eli die. It ain't been long she jus' had the kitchen gutted and redid, gearing up to have a swanky pahty about them huntahs again. She have that big fancified chandelier put in on a heavy beam. It expensive but she say it be worth every penny." She dropped her head. "I hear that where she was hanging."

"Yes, I'm afraid that's true. But, Ms. Rich, you said you cooked turkey, ham, and beef for these occasions?"

"I did 'xactly what she told me to, Miss."

"I thought she was a vegetarian."

"She be that, but she knowed the men wouldn't come unless she put on the dog, so to speak, so she allow meat just at times she have the pahties. She really jus' a hypocrite."

"Do you know who was going to attend this party?"

"Bigwigs in the county. Commissionahs, senatahs, congressmens, and she even invited the guvnah. He turn her down, and she some kind of mad about it too. I liked Mr. Eli when he livin'. He a fine man. Friends? No friends I ever see. She endure Miss Rose Paul, though. Miss Rose Paul come in some and have coffee. Yes ma'am, she have enemies. She could get real mean."

"How was she mean?"

"She got mad at me one Saerdy mornin' 'cause I throwed away crates of rotten eggs been lef' on the porch in the sun. She say she lef' 'em there to spoil. I say 'why' and she say she gone throw 'em at houses and squish some in mailboxes. Then she jus' laugh her fool head off. Them eggs some kind of rotten. I thought that woman gone coo-coo."

"Do you know any particular people she planned to target

with the eggs?"

"Anybody she don't like. Mainly huntahs around here. She hate them huntahs with a passion."

"Did she keep the house secured?" Magnolia Rich looked puzzled. "You know, locked, even when she was home?"

"She never lock nothin' 'til one Sund'y not too long ago. She start lockin' after the Sund'y she come home from church shakin'."

"What happened at church?"

"She say a whole bunch of huntahs go up in the balcony and stare at her the whole time the preacher preachin'. She say they sing out the hymns real big and look at her when certain words were used. She say they tryin' to scare her. She make out like it don't bother her, but it do too. Real bad."

"How long between the time this happened and her death?"

"Lawdy, child, I don't know. Maybe three or fo' weeks."

"So, this wasn't back during hunting season?"

"I suppose not, but they's always some poor animal being hunted around here."

"Thank you, Ms. Rich. You've been very helpful. I'll let you get back to the other ladies." I turned and then twisted back. "Oh, Ms. Rich, please don't discuss what you've just told me with anyone."

"Goodness gracious, sake's alive. Huh! They all so uppity it a pleasure to be outside away from 'em. I won't say a word even though they try to pick my bones. It be's a pleasure to keep it from 'em. And it be's a pleasure to meet you, Miss." She grinned. "You takes care of yo'self now, Miss. You so tall you need some flesh on your bones. And call me Magnolia. Everbody do."

With that, Magnolia Rich smiled and walked back toward Whiney's house.

"Yes, ma'am," I called after her.

I decided that I'd check out the church the following Sunday to see who the congregation included, out of curiosity more than anything else. I didn't have a dress with me, so heads turned when I walked in wearing my official navy pantsuit. It had been a long time since I'd been in any church, my job pulling me all over the state and crime having no respect for the Sabbath.

The exterior of the wood church had been freshly painted for Homecoming services. Three doors on the front of the porch at the top of five steps confused me, but folks went in all three. I had no idea which one to choose, so I walked through the main door in the middle.

The number of people packing into the tiny church whom I recognized surprised me. Navel Face and his wife, Woody Forbesch and, I guessed, his wife or significant other, Acme Beavers and Rachel Blanche and the children, and the Latino family from Hawk Daw's fields. I spotted Rose Paul Hill near the front. Magnolia Rich, the only black, adjusted her dress on the back pew.

I followed the crowd, some looking back at me and whispering, into the uncomfortable pews. Once seated, I looked up at the long narrow balconies that ran down both sides of the church, all the way to where the hard-looking Preacher Hawfield walked from a side door to the pulpit. He walked like a crane, his head and long neck going first, followed slowly by the rest of him. He appeared to lack energy. I might soon be hearing the most boring sermon I'd ever endured.

I had never attended any worship service like The Church of God with Signs Following, not at all like the Southern Baptist Church of my childhood. It began with a rowdy piano and tambourines. Then folks jumped up and started clapping and hollering. Those who had gone through the side doors on the porch hung over the balcony ledges on either side of the principal pews.

I sat still and observed the spirit moving in them. At least I figured that's what was going on.

Once the song ended, people settled back on the pews and Preacher Hawfield stood up with gusto he'd found somewhere during the tambourine episode and quoted scripture. I was impressed, at first, that he held no Bible or notes.

Had he memorized his message?

Then his eyes rolled back in his head, and he started saying things I couldn't understand, getting louder with each breath and more animated as he continued. I'd heard about some churches in Tennessee, Georgia, and West Virginia where people spoke in tongues, but I'd never witnessed it, and didn't know the practice existed in this part of North Carolina.

Preacher Hawfield got downright boisterous and so did the congregation. People in the balcony leaned precariously over the railing again. I expected someone to fall over and land on the first floor, so it unnerved me. I looked around for a sedate face. My eyes locked on Magnolia in the back row, and she smiled and nodded at me. Maybe she noticed my uneasiness.

I smiled back, but jumped when the preacher shouted.

"My people, let the Spirit move in you. Let it anoint you. Give over to it."

He created what I'd call a public disturbance if it happened anywhere else, but here everyone bought it. The little building trembled from the ever-increasing racket. My Southern Baptist roots were coming undone, but my SBI curiosity amped.

I turned my attention to the front of the church just in time to see Rose Paul Hill get up and start dancing toward the preacher as the music became more erotic than religious. People bumped and grinded in the pews, hands raised and yelling out all sorts of words I didn't recognize. I leaned around a giant of a man to keep my eyes on Rose Hill.

Why is she going to the front? And why is this old lady thrashing and twisting her body like a belly dancer?

"Sister Rose Paul Hill has come. Let's pray that she is anointed, my brothers and sisters."

I jumped to my feet as everyone started to look up and pray, each prayer very loud and different from the next. The prayers reached a fever pitch when the preacher handed Rose a vial, which she held up and poured down her throat. The service crescendoed as Rose Paul Hill let out a yell louder than anyone in the church. I couldn't take my eyes off her. All of a sudden her loose false teeth bounced out of her mouth and across the floor, breaking into several pieces. The room became frighteningly quiet.

Rose fell to the floor; nobody tried to catch her. I worked my way to the end of the pew and ran to the front. The preacher at first seemed delighted that the Spirit moved me—until I stopped and knelt beside Rose.

"What did you drink, Rose?"

"Strychnine."

"That's poison!"

"I'm anointed, child. It won't kill me." Rose Paul's unconvincing voice grew weak. I glanced over at her broken dentures, wondering if the dental bill would finish her off. I saw movement under the front pew and blinked several times. My eyes were clear and focused, and, more than likely, outside their sockets.

"Holy Shit!" I yelled out, snatching a raggedy old toupee off a man's head as he let out a yelp. I threw it at the snake, hoping he'd think it was an animal he could overpower.

It didn't work. The humongous snake, thicker than my upper arm, came straight toward me. I could see his beady eyes under the hairpiece as he moved swiftly across the wood floor. Grabbing the Glock from under my jacket, I aimed and shot the rattlesnake twice.

"She's got a gun!"

People started screaming and stampeding for the doors. The preacher and some of the men jumped me, wrestling the gun from me and pinning me to the wood floor. Somebody lifted Rose away from the ruckus.

"What are you doing? A snake under that pew. I killed him for you."

Preacher Hawfield shrieked into my face, "You imbecile! That snake and all the others are for this service!"

All the others?

Two hefty men escorted me out of the church, through the crowd, and deposited me in the dirt near my Hummer. One man threw my gun down beside me.

I was still on the ground when Preacher Hawfield appeared again. I thought he'd peck my face with his beak of a nose. "You're not welcome here. Don't you ever come back!"

Twelve

"Hunter?" Kent Poletti. *This can't be good.*

"Yes, sir," I responded, half asleep.

"What the hell is going on down there?"

His tone of voice had me clamoring out of my stupor.

"What do you mean, sir?"

"I just had a phone call from some irate preacher down there who woke me up after I've been out all night. He claims you shot up his church and ruined his worship service. Is that true?"

"I didn't shoot up his church. I shot the rattlesnake under the pew when I tried to help the lady who drank poison," I said.

"What?"

"I didn't know the church members drink strychnine and handle snakes. I thought I was saving them."

"The preacher failed to mention that part. What kind of church is it?"

"The Church of God with Signs Following. I guess I should have researched it before I went. I wanted to see who showed up. There was a crowd of people who taunted Clara Banoak before she was killed. I went as part of the investigation, sir."

"Well, Preacher Hawthorne..."

"Hawfield," I corrected.

Preacher Hawfield wants me to remove you from the case and get you out of their hair."

"What? No, please!"

"You wanted some time off to get married, didn't you?"

"That was before this case. Please, sir, don't take me off. I'm already deeply involved."

"Don't worry, Hunter. I just wanted to make certain you were giving 100 percent." Poletti's voice softened.

"Haven't I always?"

"You have. And the church incident has nothing to do with your murder investigation as far as I'm concerned. Just don't go back to that church."

"Don't worry about that, sir. I'll do my observing some other way."

Fully conscious at 5:30 in the morning, I dressed and headed back to Black River. On the desolate strip of highway between New Bern and Kinston, I saw the blue light. I had no idea what speed he'd clocked with his radar gun. The old geezer should have been retired anyway, from the look of him.

"License and registration, Miss."

I obliged.

He began writing me a speeding ticket for going seventy in a fifty-five but then stopped writing and looked at me with a smile. "You're a fine-looking woman."

"Thank you, Officer."

He looked up and down the highway. No traffic from east or west on this desolate strip of road. I could see this situation getting ugly.

"Why don't you step out of the vehicle and do a man a favor? I'll forget about the ticket." He unzipped his pants and grinned until I shoved my SBI badge in his face. He turned an exquisite shade of red.

"Look, asshole, I suggest you forget the ticket anyway, unless you'd like me to report this sexual harassment. And, furthermore, I'd suggest you retire as soon as you get back to your station."

He closed the ticket book, darted to his cruiser, and spun around me at a high rate of speed.

I wonder how many frightened women he's pulled that on?

After I walked the Banoak grounds again in the early daylight,
I saw a small plastic bag on the hood of the Hummer. I peered
into the warm bag and unwrapped two homemade applejacks.
A note from Magnolia Rich accompanied them:

Miss,

You's the talk of that church!

You near 'bout tickled me to death.

Enjoy these.

M

I wolfed down the delight. Then I called Chase to see when
he would join me in the investigation, and to tell him about the
church incident. I missed him something awful.

"Hello?" A woman yawned.

My heart stopped. Raina! Chase's old flame, and the most
beautiful Cherokee I'd ever seen. I closed the lid on my cell phone,
ending the call at 7:12 a.m.

It rang. I stared at Chase's name in the little data window.
How could he?

Almost a year ago he had told me he and Raina were history.
I'd shared things from my past with him I'd never shared with
anyone. Because I trusted him. He'd asked me to marry him.
And Raina spent the night?

Tears burned my cheeks and reappeared as fast as I wiped
them away. My heart was torn like a ligament detaching from
bone. Hurt seeped through every conceivable crack in my armor. The applejacks came back up. Chase, my soul mate, cheated on me while I worked a gruesome crime scene on the other
side of the state.

My cell phone continued to ring. I erased the voicemails
without playing them back. I didn't want to hear anything Chase
Railey had to say.

Thirteen

I saw him as he came around the house and headed past the graveyard toward me. My blood boiled. "What are you doing here?" I growled.

"Logan, we have to talk." Chase rubbed his hands through his hair, something he always did when stressed.

"Get the hell away from me!"

"Logan, it's not what you think."

I threw up both hands for him to shut up, glaring at him.

"Don't do this. Give me a chance to explain. You owe me that."

"Owe you? I owe you squat! I confided in you, trusted you, and loved you, you son of a bitch!" I wanted to beat him half to death with my fists. Instead I turned my back to him, blowing hot air from my lungs at an alarming rate. Eventually I heard him moving away, and when I turned around, he had disappeared. I stayed by the river long enough to sob and compose myself before heading back to the house.

Chase wasn't gone. He stood on the upstairs balcony, introducing himself to Nita Quicki. No way to avoid being seen. At least he would get some attention from Nita, who always had her claws primed to ensnare another man. I stayed clear of both of them, nearly stepping off into one of her damn holes. I stopped and looked around. The backyard looked like gophers had invaded.

I heard Quicki's convertible and Chase's Jeep leave. I was

relieved to avoid another unpleasant encounter.

Another confrontation was inevitable. Chase had been officially assigned to work with me on the Banoak case. I grumbled as I got out of the Hummer, seeing his Jeep already beside the shed on the other side of the house. I stood as tall as possible, took a deep breath, and made sure my guns were loaded. I rounded the building at a quick clip. He ducked his head under a limb and looked up at me from a crouched position.

"Good morning. Feeling better today?" I walked on past him without saying a word. "Still got a case of the ass, Logan?"

I whipped around. "Shut up! Give me a freaking break. You're the one with the ass. I believe her name is Raina."

He jumped to his feet, his face reddening. "Logan, you're breaking my heart here. I can explain. I didn't sleep with her. She..."

"Please spare me the lies. I don't want to hear any of it. Get the hell out of here."

"Not happening, Logan. Like it or not, I'm assigned to help you with this case. You might as well resign yourself to that. We can get this case solved much quicker together."

"You don't think I can handle it on my own?"

"Don't put words in my mouth. You know what I mean."

"I've done most of the investigating. There's very little for you to do." I lied. I needed all the help I could get.

"You've got a prime suspect?"

"Several, but I'm gradually discounting some of them."

"Okay, where should I start?" Chase, eager to make amends and take all the information I'd gathered on my own, bounced on his toes.

"Not so fast, Hot Shot. Dig up your own information. I'm not feeling very generous."

"You can't be serious. You'd let a murderer get away just to get back at me for...for something I didn't even do? Well, I don't know you as well as I thought, Logan Hunter." His face filled with sweat and he wiped it with his shirtsleeve, staring at me all the while.

I was demoralized by all of this, but he had a good point: I couldn't let a killer get away just to get back at Chase. But I wasn't admitting that to him.

"Can I, at least, ask you where you sleep at night? I didn't see any hotels. Not even campgrounds. This place is in the boonies."

"You'll have to sleep in your Jeep, or maybe on the screened porch on the side of the house. Don't worry. The nights are dazzling. The river breeze is peaceful." I lied again, knowing more than he did about the humid, sticky nights near the river's edge.

We separated and spent the day wandering around trying to avoid each other. Since I felt no benevolence toward Chase, I hid my notes and gave him Yonder Store as a possible point of interest.

Dusk arrived and quickly turned to pitch darkness as I headed down the road past Yonder Store, taking the next road, and heading to the beach for some solitude and distance.

Fourteen

When I reached the crime scene the next day, I barely recognized Chase, one gigantic red welt, almost eaten alive by shit flies and what the locals called Teeth. I choked down a laugh, but he could tell I'd done it on purpose.

"There's nothing funny about this, Logan." He scratched everywhere he could scratch. "I'm assuming you had a better sleeping arrangement."

I said nothing. I walked to the Hummer and retrieved a tube of After Bug cream and threw it to him. Then I drove off with an evil laugh as he slathered it on. The guilt hit a few minutes later, but I tried to ignore it.

When the rain started coming down in buckets, I circled the snake church and headed for Yonder Store to see if Navel Face had any fresh pre-packaged sandwiches. There were more cars there than usual, so I couldn't park close. I fumbled around behind the seat and grabbed the yellow umbrella my little cousin had forgotten weeks before. I stepped out and opened the umbrella, running toward the door. Just as I reached it, a grinning Sly Foxx swung it open. I maneuvered around him, staring into amused faces as laughter broke out around me and got increasingly louder. Chase, in my direct line of vision, seemed stuck somewhere between muffled laughter and stunned silence.

I turned back to Sly, laughing loudest.

"Haven't you ever seen a woman with an umbrella?"

"Not like that," he said, slapping his leg. I'd paid no attention to the umbrella. I pulled it down to eye level. The main shoots were bright yellow. The front had an orange duckbill, and two movable eyes stared back at me from above the bill. *Crap!* I felt the blush of embarrassment but decided I might as well laugh at myself. Cute for a five-year-old, but not for an SBI agent who needed to be taken seriously.

"It did keep me dry." I tried to regain some dignity. I gave Chase a quick look. He frowned and walked to the back of the store.

I drove back to the Banoak house and put on my heavy rain gear: yellow overalls with suspenders, a jacket and hood, and seventeen-inch slush boots. I stuck my Armor gloves in a pocket and made sure my gun was strapped outside, easily accessible.

Who needs a frigging umbrella anyway?

Sly drove up about then. I was glad I'd had time to get into official rain gear before he came.

"Sexy outfit, if I may say so, Agent Hunter."

"Look…"

"I came to apologize for laughing at you in front of all those men. I shouldn't have." He moved closer. "A cute umbrella, I have to admit." His pouty lips curled a little.

I found myself smiling back.

He handed me a Snickers and a Pepsi.

"These I bought in Atkinson. They're fresh."

"Apology accepted, I suppose."

"I know it's important for you to be taken seriously. I didn't mean to…"

"I know. I didn't even realize it was a duck." We both giggled.

"Let me make it up to you then. How about we ride to Wilmington and get a pig in a puppy and a couple of beers?"

"Sly, I don't think so. I've got too much crap going on right now. Thanks anyway."

"You and Railey?"

I pulled my shoulders back. "Is it that obvious?"

"Right off-hand, I'd say your relationship with Agent Railey is far more than just two agents working a case together. But who could blame him? You..."

"Don't! I don't want to talk about this!" I stomped off in my cute yellow rain suit.

Sly called out, "Maybe some other time."

I didn't look back.

Hard rain continued for three days. I felt moldy from the top of my head to the bottom of my feet. The whole world mildewed, making me miserable. I couldn't investigate squat in this mess, even with rain-appropriate gear—and any unclaimed speck of evidence had already washed away. The one thing I could do in the monsoon was interview anyone left on my list who might have known Clara Banoak or who may have overheard some talk about the murder. Maybe someone was bragging by now.

I wanted to check on Rose Paul Hill since her encounter with the poison, so I stopped in her driveway and waited for the downpour to become a drizzle. I ate my Scotchman roasted chicken sandwich and bag of cheese sticks with my water. After wiping the crumbs, I approached the door.

"Agent Hunter, I wondered when you were coming in. I saw you sitting in the driveway. Come on back," she said, leading me into the house.

"I don't want to disturb you, Rose Paul, but I was concerned about your drinking that poison."

"I'm fine," she clacked. "Well, except for these aggravating teeth." She grinned, showing two teeth missing from her front denture. "I was out of kilter for a few days, but I got over it all right."

"I wondered if you could even wear your teeth again." I stifled a giggle. She looked like an old hillbilly from a Hee-Haw re-run.

"I don't have dental insurance, so these will have to do. I bought some straws," she said, pointing to a tall clear glass filled with bendable straws in pretty colors.

"That can't be all bad, I suppose."

"Agent Hunter, I know you don't understand all our ways, but we're good people. Most of us, at least." She peered into my face. "And what on earth possessed you to go to the church in the first place?"

"I just wanted to observe some people important to the case, Rose Paul. I didn't have any idea we had those kinds of churches in this part of the country."

"We didn't until the Hawfields moved here. He kind of moved our Pentecostal Holiness Church in that direction. We were curious about being anointed and letting the Spirit move in us. Some people left, but many others came. You saw how full the church was. There's no pressure to handle snakes or drink poison. In fact, I had no idea I'd do that until the Spirit touched me and marched me to the front. It's all in a haze."

"I'm just glad you're okay," I said, patting her knee. "Listen, did you ever get new Christmas bulbs for your front porch?"

"Yes, but I'm afraid to climb the ladder, and I haven't found a man to do it."

"Get them for me, and I'll get the ladder since it's stopped raining." She let out a delighted squeal and danced a little jig.

"Oh, that would be super! The ladder is leaning up against the back of the house."

I moved the ladder around to the porch while she turned on the lights so I could find the bad ones. I removed each burned-out bulb, one at a time, and replaced it with a new one as she handed it up to me. We stood back and admired them before going in for a cup of cider and two sugar cookies.

After taking the last sip of my cider, I stood up. "I've got to go. Take care of yourself, Rose Paul."

"Thanks for checking on me, Agent Hunter. And thanks for fixing those lights. Maybe they'll all last through New Year's."

I checked my voicemail for the first time that day. "Agent Hunter, I need to see you," Cy said. "I got your cell number from the sheriff. Call me back as fast as you can. It's urgent. Please! It's about ten o'clock in the morning." It was now nearly four o'clock. His voice sounded anxious and troubled, very unlike Cy.

Maybe he'd had too much to drink. But even though people called him an alcoholic and a dextro head, I'd never heard him slur his speech, and, somehow, I liked him in spite of his short-comings. I just couldn't help myself. I didn't think he was Clara's killer. He probably wasn't involved on any level. That made him an outsider—like me.

I dialed his number and got no answer. I drove over to his place to park beside his truck, and as I pulled up, the horses ran out of the barn and toward the blueberry fields. *How odd.* I didn't see Cy at the barn, but I walked in. Nobody.

Had he binged and let the horses out?

I heard his basset hound, Homer, baying out back of the house. I soon knocked on the wreathed front door, but Cy didn't answer it. I turned the knob and entered. I'd been all over the house calling for him, and was about to leave when I saw him on the ground behind the house.

"Cy!" I ran to him. I checked for a pulse on his cold skin. None. A Wild Turkey bottle lay close by. I whiffed the bottle and poured some of the liquid on the ground. Whiskey. He was used to drinking whiskey.

Did he have a heart attack? A stroke? Or had someone put poison in his whiskey bottle, knowing he was an alcoholic, and knowing he was trying to help me find Clara Banoak's killer? Did he know something about the murder that got him killed?

Homer threw his head back and wailed the most mournful sound I'd heard in years. He pulled on his chain, nearly chok-ing, as he tried in vain to reach his master. I approached the dog and cupped my hand, barely moving it closer in order to win his trust. He sniffed it and wagged his tail. I moved my hand slowly and patted his head, not wanting to lose any digits in the process. Homer let me scratch between his ears, so I comforted the agitated dog as best I could while I dialed the sheriff.

The team arrived and we scoured the ground and yard for evidence of foul play. Lemmie examined the body and was about to drive Cyrano Blood away from his home for the last time when I walked back to the whimpering dog.

I surveyed the chain and discovered it fastened not with a lock but some fandangled conglomeration of twisted links. Having gained Homer's trust, I worked to give him the freedom to go to his master. The chain loosened, and I had to hold on to the hound with a tight grip so he wouldn't choke himself. He licked me on the face as I felt the chain lose its tautness, and I eased it off his collar. He sprang to his master, lying too still on the gurney. Homer howled louder, with great sorrow as I, too, succumbed to mournful sobs.

I heard the crunch of leaves as someone walked up behind me. I turned quickly, sticking my Glock in Chase's solemn face. I wiped my eyes and turned back toward Cy. Chase put his arms around me, and I didn't pull away. I needed to be held, and as much as it hurt to admit, I needed Chase to hold me. I tried to choke back my sobs and realized Chase's eyes were full of tears too.

"Wh-why are you crying? You didn't even know him."

"When you hurt, I hurt, Logan. And you're definitely in pain." Having said that, Chase turned and walked off toward his Jeep.

You're damn right I'm hurting.

I sat down on the ground beside Cy and bawled until I wore myself out. Lemmie and Sheriff Gunn stood by silently, letting me get it all out. I stayed there until Lemmie motioned to take Cy's body away. Reluctantly I moved away after patting the body bag.

I was incensed that someone might have taken Cy's life. He had called to tell me something he'd found out about Clara's murder. I knew it. And somebody must have stopped him from getting the message to me. But I had no idea what news he might have had. I walked back through the house, checking to see if anything was out of place, or if Cy laid anything out to show me. I didn't have any idea what to look for. I went through his old truck, but found nothing but layers of dust, dirt, and rust, even on the inside.

The saddest part was fully understanding what a good man Cy was. Misunderstood, but first-rate by any decent human's measurement.

And what would become of Homer?

After I regained some degree of composure, I drove back to the Banoak property. As I got out of my Hummer, I saw Chase limping across the yard in noticeable pain.

"What happened to you?"

"Somebody's been digging holes in the yard. I stepped in a deep one before I noticed it. Turned my ankle, I think."

I yanked my first-aid kit from the back and opened it in front of him.

"I'm fine, Logan. Just leave me the hell alone."

"No, you're not fine. Let me check it."

"Are you a doctor now?"

"Chase, for Pete's sake! I'm trying to be civil." I pulled up his pants leg and saw a badly swollen ankle, already deep purple. "I think you did more than turn it, Chase."

"Ouch! Don't touch it so hard." He hobbled to a nearby bench, and I moved with him.

I took another look. "You need ice on this right away, but I'm not sure we can find any. I think you need to have it x-rayed."

"Yeah? Where? Over there in that shed? How about that row of mossy trees over there, or even Yonder Store?"

"Funny. I can drive you to Burgaw. That's the nearest hospital, I guess."

"No. I'm fine. Leave it alone." He stood up, turned white, and sat back down. Then he turned his head and puked right beside my shoe.

"Can I help you now, Thick Skull?"

Chase let out a long angry sigh. "Well, I suppose you have

the time now that the killer's dead."

"What?" I came close to biting his nose off. "What are you talking about? You just got here, and you already know so much that you're accusing Cy?"

"Seems likely to me. Everybody I've talked to says Blood and Banoak were enemies."

"No. No, Chase. Cy didn't do it." I clenched my teeth and my fist.

"Logan, you can't come in here in a few days and know these people well enough to be certain," Chase said.

"I'm telling you I know Cyrano Blood didn't do it. He, like hundreds of others, didn't care for Clara Banoak, but he didn't have the heart to kill." I believed that even if nobody else did.

I helped Chase into the Hummer without another word and drove him to the hospital's ER. X-rays indicated a severely sprained ankle. The doctor strapped him into an awkward plastic ankle brace, we purchased a pair of crutches at the local pharmacy, filled his prescription, and headed to my place at the beach.

"What makes you think I'm staying with you after the way you've treated me?"

"The way I treated *you*? You've got to be kidding me!"

"Logan, I didn't cheat on you!"

"Just shut up, Chase."

I didn't believe a word of it, glad he was in pain. Kinda. He reclined his seat and was soon dead to the world, I supposed due to the medication and sheer exhaustion from hobbling around most of the day. I'd been on crutches before and remembered they could beat you half to death.

We got to my place, and I helped Chase out even though I could tell he would be a dreadful patient.

I settled him in the Barcalounger I seldom sat in, and got him a glass of water. Time for more pain medicine.

When I handed it to him, he held on to my hand. "Logan, I'm sorry about this, and what I said about Mr. Blood back there. I shouldn't have said such a thing. I know you don't want me here. I'm fine. Tomorrow you need to take me back to the crime scene and my Jeep."

"If you don't stay here, where will you stay?"

"I heard there's a motel around there somewhere."

I had to laugh. "The Azalea Motel? You can't be serious!" He looked puzzled. "Have you seen it, Chase?"

"No."

"It's torn all to pieces for renovation."

"Then my Jeep will have to do."

"Or, you can stay here," I said. He looked up. "For a few days, I mean."

"No, Logan, I don't want to."

With that, I headed for the kitchen. I threw together a salad and opened a can of tuna. I busied myself while the eggs boiled. *My* eggs boiled too. Here I was at my own home, with the man who'd cheated on me.

Why had I brought him home with me? Why hadn't I left him at the hospital so some family member could take responsibility?

I slammed the hot eggs into the sink and ran cold water over them.

Why? Because, damn it, I love him. Love him in spite of the fact that he has hurt me terribly, in spite of the fact he's destroyed my trust in him.

I sulked and completed the preparations, deciding to brown a few buttered rolls to go with the tuna and salad.

I got the table set and glanced at the recliner, cranked back as far as it would go, Chase's feet in the air, a light snore coming from his mouth.

I sat down and ate, watching him and wishing things were different. Wanting to go back to before the phone call. Wishing I'd never met Raina. I realized then how much time I spent every day trying to figure out who lied and who didn't. I ate all four rolls before I realized it.

Hours went by, and Chase never stirred. I put a blanket over him and went into my bedroom. I pulled a few Christmas decorations out of a closet, but then dropped them on the floor. I was nowhere near a festive mood.

The following morning Chase could barely move, even with the crutches, so rather than leave him alone in a strange place, I stayed with him begrudgingly, calling Sheriff Gunn a few times during the day. Chase slept most of the time and I thoroughly cleaned the condominium for the first time in a long time.

By suppertime, he ate a big plate of spaghetti, a small salad, and some homemade bread. We had little to say to each other. I walked the beach and then we watched a movie, Chase in the den and me in the bedroom. I decided to make one thing perfectly clear before I went to bed, so I stood in the den doorway.

"We'll be going back in the morning. Cy's funeral is tomorrow. I wouldn't miss it…for anyone." I moved into the bedroom before looking back at him. "And what are you planning to do about your Jeep? You busted your right ankle. You can't drive."

"Sure I can. I'll figure it out," he snarled.

Gunn called that the toxicology report confirmed Cy's Wild Turkey contained a lethal dose of antifreeze. Because it was clear, colorless, and odorless, Cyrano ingested a deadly amount that caused renal failure as well as widespread liver, brain, and kidney damage. I fumed, eaten up with guilt because I knew what a good man Cyrano Blood was. I knew he'd called to tell me something crucial about the case. It had taken me hours to respond, crucial hours that Cy didn't have. If only I had checked my cell phone, or better yet, answered the call. I didn't even have a good excuse. I knew I'd be forever haunted by his death.

A large number of people attended Cyrano's graveside funeral, including Ogden Gunn, Lemmie Sawyer, Hawk Daw, Sly Foxx, Navel Face from Yonder Store and his wife, one cousin, me, and even Chase, standing awkwardly with his crutches at a considerable distance from me.

We hadn't had much to say since he awoke, took a shower,

and hobbled to the Hummer. The tension between us was merciless. The silence felt like a vacuum in my broken heart, splayed open by betrayal, and now enormous guilt. The Banoak crime scene had been compromised from the beginning—Chase, cheated on me—and Cyrano Blood was dead. And maybe somehow, it had been my fault.

I refocused on the funeral service and the preacher delivering the eulogy.

"He carried food, or any animals he hunted, to sick and elderly people all over the county, often times cooking it himself before he delivered it," explained the preacher. Some of the crowd nodded. "Some of you may not have known what a good cook Cyrano was." He smiled and paused as reflection momentarily halted his eulogy. "I've had the pleasure, on many occasions, of joining him for supper. A fine cook, and proud of his culinary dishes as well as his needlework.

"On the job, he always made the biggest contributions to fundraisers, even though he tried to do things anonymously. He was also the county's coordinator for the Make a Wish Foundation, making dreams come true for children with life-threatening illnesses. They will be challenged to find another as benevolent as Cyrano Blood."

Many of the people standing near the grave seemed surprised at how little they knew about him, especially those who'd lived near him all their lives. Perhaps I'd come to know him better in a few weeks than most of them had in a lifetime. It was such a shame. I would miss his old scruffy face and big blue eyes. And the grin that hauled me in every time I was around him.

The preacher said Cy had taken to liquor after his wife died with cancer, and his daughter, and only child, died in a fiery car crash on a Thanksgiving Day. Cy had always blamed himself for not getting around to buying new tires. After her death, he got drunk every year on that holiday.

"I blame myself in some ways for not checking up on him. For not dropping by on Thanksgiving Day this year—or the days since—to share a tale or two with an old friend," the preacher added, his face mournful.

We all left the gravesite with heads hanging low. I was miserable. And some of the mourners seemed ashamed of how they'd alienated Cyrano Blood just because he had been a little different.

Sheriff Gunn nudged my elbow. "Who's that man over there by the trees? I saw him with you in Cyrano's yard."

"That's Agent Railey. He's on the case now." I had no desire to say more. Gunn nodded and strolled over to introduce himself to Chase. I stayed back.

Hawk Daw walked up to me after the final prayer. "Agent Hunter? I just wanted you to know I liked Cy. Even though he was kinda scary-looking, he had a big heart. Why, he'd kill a deer, maybe keep some tenderloin, and take the rest to a poor family with four or five kids to feed, just like the preacher said. He'd kill a few quail when he could find them, save two, and give the rest away. He volunteered with Hunters for the Hungry too.

"But I didn't know about all the other good stuff he did. More of us need to get involved in good causes, I expect. I'm sorry he's dead. I'm feeling pretty rotten right now about some things I said about him."

I nodded and walked away. What could I say?

Sly called out for me to come by his house later as I heard a muffled rendition of "When the Saints Go Marching In" coming from someone's cell phone. It wasn't mine, but the song did seem to fit the occasion. I looked at Chase shuffling just ahead of me toward the Hummer, struggling with the crutches on uneven terrain. I saw the phone in the moss. Chase must have dropped it. It continued to ring as I opened it up.

"Hello, Chase? Look, this is Raina. Thanks again for letting me stay at your place when Efrain stalked me. I got a restraining order against him, but I need you to come on the court date if you can. By the way, I hope you worked out the misunderstanding with Agent Hunter. I know you love her. I hope she knows how lucky she is. Can you come for court?"

"R...Raina?" I stuttered. "This is Logan Hunter." I didn't recognize my own voice.

"Agent Hunter, is that you? There's static on the line. How are things going?"

"Not too well." I took a deep breath. "Listen, I need to know."

"What?"

"I need to know if you slept with Chase. Please, just tell me the truth."

"Agent Hunter, Chase tried to call you back several times. But, no. I mean, I didn't have sex with him. I was willing, but he wasn't. He's pitifully in love with you, not me. I had my chance and blew it.

"And now I have my own trouble. This mad man has been stalking me. My car broke down on the highway near Chase's house. I was hysterical by the time he came home. He insisted I stay. I slept in his bed. He stayed on the futon. I swear to you, he never touched me. I hope you believe me.

"Agent Hunter, take good care of him, you hear? He's one of the nicest men I've ever met."

"Thank you, Raina." I pushed OFF, hugged the phone to my chest, and cried softly, wanting to let out a barrage of pent-up emotions. But somehow I couldn't. Not yet. I felt relief, but I wasn't ready to talk to Chase. I'd just let him stew a while longer while I decided what to say and how to make it up to him.

Fifteen

I met the familiar truck, recognizing Hawk Daw's son, Ethan, driving alone again. I waved but he seemed to duck and drive by me, perhaps because he knew he drove illegally.

I turned around and followed, keeping him in sight from a distance. I don't know why exactly. I just felt the need to do it. He soon braked and turned into a sandy path that led to the river.

I waited a few minutes. When he didn't come out, I parked and walked in, the trees my cover. I felt bad for being nosy, but it seemed odd for him to be here at this time of day, and to be driving without his dad. Maybe Hawk allowed him to go fishing by himself, but an ominous sensation tightened around something in my guts that I couldn't yet identify.

I recognized Nita Quicki's convertible in thick trees and brush. Unfortunately, Ethan had positioned his dad's truck where I couldn't see either of them. I couldn't figure out why Ethan would be meeting Nita here—or any place, for that matter. Maybe Nita hired him to gather pine straw or help her with some kind of chore. But why the need for secrecy?

My radio squawked, and I stooped, looking up to see if they'd spotted me. They hadn't. I eased back to the Hummer with my curiosity more stimulated than satisfied. I got in, but didn't close the door. I sat there for a second. When my inquisitiveness overwhelmed me, I placed the radio on the seat and got back out.

When I glimpsed them through the trees again, Nita kissed Ethan. Not a peck on the cheek kiss, but a full-on-the-mouth passionate kiss. My mouth flew open long enough for an insect to fly in. I sputtered, covering my mouth and ducking, just in case they heard me. I spit out the nasty bug, now wet and withered. *It serves him right.* I eased back into a standing position and took another look. They stopped kissing and started talking, Nita mostly, with her hands very animated. She seemed excited, and Ethan was getting there. Their voices got louder, but from a distance I couldn't hear what they were saying over the truck radio's infernal music.

When they appeared to be leaving, I ran to the Hummer and left before they discovered they hadn't been alone. What I witnessed troubled me. I wrestled with the notion of going to Hawk with my discovery, but I choked back the opportunity to tattletale.

But would I be a tattletale or simply a concerned investigator?

I decided to wait and watch, to find out what Nita was up to. I knew she had to be seducing Ethan for some reason. If I said something now, I'd never know what was going on between this fifteen-year-old kid and the mid-forties daughter of the murder victim.

I drove down the state road, heading farther away from Nita, Ethan, and the Banoak property. I spotted a multitude of cars and trucks down another path to the river.

What now?

Maybe someone got married down by the river, or perhaps it was a church baptism like they had years ago, before churches built pools into the back of the pulpit. My curiosity overtaking me, I pulled in to witness an old-timey church tradition. I hopped out and walked around all the vehicles before my feet froze in place. Naked. Naked butts. Naked fronts. Perky boobs. Saggy boobs. Flaccid penises. Erect penises. No clothes whatsoever. This was no church baptism. It was a river nudist colony!

"Well, well. Heidi, ma'am," came a man's voice to my right. Before I thought, I looked. *Boing!* My eyes gazed upon a penis, alive and moving upward.

"Whoa!"

"Ain't you ever seen a penis afore?"

"Sir, I'm trying not to look, but you're making it very difficult."

"Just call me Bic Dick 'cause I can take a licking and…"

"Spare me the rest of that sentence," I said moving back toward the Hummer.

He took several more steps toward me.

"Yeah. Big, ain't it? I been blessed, that's for shor." He grinned and kept coming.

"Mine's bigger," I said, whipping out my Glock.

"Easy there, Girlie. Just making polite conversation. But since you're nasty, I'm leaving."

Yeah, take a hint!

The man toddled off to several naked women who seemed to be eager for his return. I eased back to the Hummer and drove toward Sly's house, having had enough surprises for one day.

Sly Foxx waved me into his yard as I drove by. I hesitated, but the yard full of people and vehicles of every description piqued my interest. At least I wouldn't be uncomfortably alone with him. My nostrils curved up into a smile. The unmistakable aroma of eastern North Carolina barbeque filled the air.

"Agent Hunter, you look like you could use a plate of grub." I smiled. "Today's my mother's birthday, so I threw a hog on the fire." He shoved a Chinette platter at me. "Here, fill this up. I'll get you a Pepsi."

I ladled slaw and boiled potatoes on my plate and walked to the pig cooker, where Sly forked up a huge piece of tenderloin onto my plate and handed me a drink from the cooler.

"I can't remember the last time I picked a pig. Chopped pig just isn't the same, is it?"

"No, it's not." He pushed back the longer red curls covering the crown of his head. "Have you found out what happened to Cyrano?" I shook my head. "Ole Cy had plenty of good qualities, I'm told. I didn't get to know him too well, even though I've lived here all my life."

"That's your loss, Sly."

"Yeah."

He pointed at a table and I dug in as the rest of the family came bounding out of the house and fixed their plates. I hadn't noticed I got my plate before the birthday girl, Sly's mother, a fine-looking redhead herself. She joined me, and I introduced myself as others sat down. Someone said grace and I ate with abandon.

Once I finished, a piece of chocolate layer cake appeared over my shoulder as I stood to go.

"Where you going? You haven't touched your cake." Sly headed in my direction with his own plate, apparently planning to sit by me.

"I better go. My partner, Agent Railey, is waiting for me."

Well, not exactly.

"Oh. I hoped we could spend some time together. You know, off the clock, after my relatives leave." His face turned a darker red than his hair. I must have looked shocked. He continued. "My girlfriend and I broke up. She moved out. We've been having problems for a while."

I hope I'm not the cause of that.

"Umm," I, too, felt a blush rising, "I thought you were involved and she lived with you." I nodded my head toward his house.

"Not anymore. It wouldn't ever have worked out. We're too different." He kept looking at me. I guess I stared back, not knowing what to say. "Well, here. Take the other agent a plate," he offered. I didn't discourage that, so I left with a heaping plate of barbeque and all the fixin's, and two Pepsis. Some lady wrapped two pieces of cake and placed them on top of a plate.

"Thank you so much. It was delicious. Tell your mom I hope her day is tremendously special." Sly opened the Hummer door for me and waved me away with pouty lips.

Chase beamed when he saw me carrying a plate of country food as a peace offering. He ate while we squabbled over whether western North Carolina tomato-paste barbeque was better than vinegar-based eastern North Carolina barbeque. I knew the truth—eastern by ten country miles. No contest. We didn't discuss our *real* problem.

After eating my cake and watching Chase wolf down his meal, I tramped through the mulch and debris around a low place on the riverbank a mile or so from the Banoak property. I ducked under some low-hanging Spanish moss and stepped into the edge of the water far enough to look up and down the river.

Out of nowhere, a loud blast from behind me nearly deafened me, and a heavy weight hit my shoulders before I could turn. Writhing wildly, I screamed, knocking the water moccasin off me and into the river, his head split open. I stood there shaking as Chase approached without his crutches.

"Thanks," I whispered. *I think.*

"My pleasure, but it wasn't my intention to drop him on you. I'm sorry I scared you and made a bloody mess of your shirt, but he was about to drop on you."

"Thanks for not blowing off an ear."

He laughed weakly. I couldn't seem to bring up laughter from anywhere in my soul. I didn't know what else to say, so I said nothing.

"What are you looking for? Can I help?" He waded into the river near me.

"I don't know what I'm looking for. I'm so tired of this fricking case, Chase," I said, splashing both hands in the river. "Most of the trace was of no use. Every man in this county has hunting knives and skinners and gambrels. And everybody hated Clara Banoak. I don't know if we'll ever know who killed that woman." I turned to look at him. "By the way, where are your crutches?"

"I'm better off without those damn things. They're just slowing me down. The ankle's doing great. Besides, maybe the water will be good for it." He smiled. "Logan, you've been through so much lately, please let me help. I can be a fresh pair of eyes, at least." I drew my gun and pointed it in his direction.

"Hey! What's with you? You don't have to be so damn hostile!"

"Don't move. Don't even twitch." Chase started to protest while I took aim and shot the moccasin right next to his leg.

"Well?" I arrogantly blew a puff of air toward the end of my Glock. "We must have disturbed a whole nest of snakes."

"Nice shot. But, Logan?"

"Huh?"

"I just creamed in my britches."

I grinned. "That makes two of us. Let's get the hell out of this infested quagmire." I thought snakes moved away from noise. So much for that thought.

And don't they hibernate? It must be the warm fall that's keeping them out.

I jumped toward the bank, and Chase pulled me up into his arms. It felt so good. I looked up into his gorgeous eyes.

"I've got an extra pair of lacy panties if you need them," I said.

"I have some jockeys in the Jeep, thanks. I'd rather see the panties on you." I wrapped my arms around him and met his lips. We held on as though we could never let go.

"God, I've missed you," we whispered simultaneously. I instantly felt stronger. I was about to tell him I'd talked to Raina, but he ruined the moment by starting the conversation.

"Logan, you know I love you. I've had my pick of girls since fourteen, and none compare to you. You're my strength, my happiness, and my balance. I'd never hurt you. But how can this work if you don't trust me?"

I couldn't respond. Something stuck in my throat. Cold, stale crow, perhaps?

"Remember when we first met, how much we laughed, even

though we had a terrible situation to deal with? Remember when you confided in me about the date rape in high school and asked me to be patient with you? Well, I'm trying, Logan, but I'm only human. We're both passionate about our jobs, and I thought we were just as passionate about each other. I hoped you'd have the courage to leave the past behind. I promised you then I'd never hurt you. Not physically, not mentally, not emotionally. Have faith in me, Logan."

With that, Chase left me standing there with my heart in my throat, wanting to say so much and not being capable of it.

Sixteen

Chase left in his Jeep to scout out another section of the river-bank while I went to Acme's to check on Cy's horses. The cousin who said he'd pick them up in a few days never came for them. Acme reluctantly agreed to keep them in his barn until the county could make arrangements, even though Cy didn't live far from him. Acme and his family were not home, so I went to the barn and checked each stall, making sure hay, oats, and plenty of water were accessible. I hoped Acme wouldn't mind. I stroked Sis's mane and talked to all five of them for a few minutes before I threw my hand up to stop a tickle on my neck. A hornet buzzed away. I looked up at the loft rafters and saw the nest, too high to reach.

I also noticed a white powder sifting through the loft boards. Acme must have stored fertilizer up there. I brushed the white powder from my shoulders and started to leave the barn. Pausing at the loft ladder, some feeling urged me to climb up and steal a look. I eased up one foot at a time, looking back to make sure Acme didn't pull in and catch me not minding my own business.

My eyes peered over the edge of the loft floor, and I all but fell backwards. I'm certain my eyes flew out of their sockets and then withdrew as far as disbelief would allow them. Bones. Hair. Teeth. What I'd thought looked like fertilizer turned out to be lime to keep down odor and rodents.

I climbed down once my feet let me, and ran to the Hummer

to call Sheriff Gunn. As I dialed the number, pain invaded my eye and the world went dark.

Bound in tight rope, I couldn't move either hand, and my legs had been bent under me long enough for them to hurt. But unbearable pain came from my left eye, where someone had punched me. Swollen shut. The contact in my eye felt like broken chips of glass grinding into my eyeball. I tried to focus with my right eye, but it was too dark. Yet, I was in some kind of wooden box.

A coffin? Oh, my God! Have I been buried alive? Has my night terror come true?

I could breathe freely and hear the hum of insects around me. I was in a box, but not underground. Outside. I wiggled and twisted enough to feel the box wobble a little. I heard a noise that I should recognize. A rattle. In the box with me.

A rattlesnake?

Motionless now, I held my breath as long as I could, afraid any noise or movement would be the end of me. Sweat poured down my body as both nipples contracted.

I was powerless against the night filled with all manner of flying insects with sharpened beaks and stingers. The Teeth everyone talked about attacked me in mass quantities. I couldn't wince, scratch, or move a muscle, terrified the snake, coiled and waiting, would strike. My eye throbbed. My parched throat constricted. My breathing became ragged due to my attempts to keep it slow and soundless. Tears dripped. I had no way to stop them.

I willed myself to think about Chase, how it felt to be in his arms again. Temporarily secure. I'd never realized how much even casual caresses meant. They were powerful and sustaining. With those thoughts to calm me, I drifted into oblivion, where nothing else could hurt me.

Seventeen

I opened my right eye as much as possible into the sunbeam as it peeked through a slit in my wooden prison. My left eye struggled to open but couldn't. It felt like a balloon attached to my face. Blood dried on my shirt and shorts, and my legs were covered with welts the size of eggs. I glanced around the box with my good eye, half-swollen shut by insect bites. I didn't see the snake.

Has it slithered away? Or is it snuggled up next to me?

I broke into a sweat. A spider moved through the sunbeam, repairing the web, no doubt, destroyed when someone threw me in here.

I wanted to move. I *had* to move. I figured I had two choices: sit here and rot or wage war. I flopped over on my side to get off my screaming knees. I listened. I didn't hear a rattle. Poisonous fangs hadn't struck me. I heard nothing but infernal insects still buzzing around my head. I started kicking my bound feet as hard as I could on the wood floor and the closest wall.

A board loosened and gave me encouragement. With all the force I could muster with bound arms and legs, I slammed both feet into the board. When it fell off, I heard a splash. A wood box over water. Not good. Maybe a dilapidated deer stand. I'd seen many in fields, marshes, and swamps. But fat chance anyone would find me. I had to get myself out. I checked the space again for the snake. I couldn't find him. I couldn't decide if that discovery relieved or unnerved me.

I continued to kick my legs until another board tore loose, dangled, and dropped with another splash. Through the swollen good eye, I saw a sharp nail pointing at me. Crawling to it on my elbows, I raised my legs and sawed. The rope was in good shape. I sawed. I rested. I sawed some more. I rested again. I sawed with determination until the thick rope began to fray and weaken, allowing me to pull my legs free.

Feeling liberated, I got on my knees and tried to stand, but I was too wobbly and faint at first. I rested a second and cleared my head. I stood up and bumped my head on the roof, covered with some type of rotting tarp. My head spun with dizziness and pain. I crouched for another minute.

When the adrenalin kicked in, I tottered over to the nail and backed up to cut my hands free. I sawed my arms back and forth, resting when necessary, until the rope weakened. I pulled my hands free and looked them over. Raw and bloody, but it felt wonderful to have them loose.

I looked out the opening into the swamp where I'd been left, a rickety deer stand my would-be coffin. The water looked still and murky. Insects buzzed constantly. I noticed a beautiful monarch butterfly alighting on a dead leaf attached to water-sucking alligator weed.

Beauty in Hell Swamp. Go figure.

With renewed zeal and a holler, I jumped, landing with a thud in the muddy swamp. I slogged and hollered my way through the putrid green, slime-filled water, hoping to find a nearby highway.

The sun, still in the east made me squint. I could make out white puffy clouds above me. At least it wouldn't rain on me. I struggled along, watching every step, and stopping often to let waves of dizziness and nausea pass. I reached out toward a cow lily, but pulled my hand back as a plump bumblebee emerged from the petals.

My better eye focused on something round floating on the scummy water. I approached it, trying to determine if some kind of swamp gas bubble had formed it. I hesitantly flipped it over. My hand shot off as I recognized the skull as human. I trembled, my stilled nerves having betrayed me. I became a heap of pitiful sobs but managed to stay on my feet and plod along.

A fog settled over the swamp water, allowing me to see only the dark silhouettes of trees some distance across the horizon. Still a considerable distance away.

I thought I heard voices. I stopped and listened. Only birds. My imagination worked over time. I thrashed on through the thick brush and mud, heading away from the water and toward civilization, I hoped.

I stopped again. I knew I heard a voice. No, I heard men's voices.

I needed to hide, but I was in the open, too far from any cover, wobbling around, and wholly vulnerable.

"Logan! My God!"

Chase sloshed toward me as best he could, considering the terrain, gathering me in his arms. I clung as I'd never clung before. Chase scooped me up, and Ogden Gunn took my long, muddy legs. They worked their way back to Gunn's cruiser, and Chase and I got in the back seat as Gunn turned on the siren and sped to the hospital in Burgaw.

I couldn't do anything but whimper, my mouth, swollen shut. Chase kept repeating, "I'll get the bastard who did this to you."

Dr. Eakins examined me thoroughly, every nook, every cranny. No broken bones. Purple gook covered every welt to help with swelling, burning, and itching. She injected my arms and buttocks with an array of shots to keep me from getting malaria, tetanus, and other horrible illnesses. I pressed an ice pack on and off my mouth and left eye every few minutes. The biggest concern, the doctor informed me—my eye, swollen shut with the contact lens broken inside. She removed the tiny shards with a suctioning device not much bigger than a match. Not yet sure how much the glass had damaged my eye, she felt certain I had no damage to the cornea itself. She also said I might experience short-term amnesia from the punch.

"How did you know where to look, Chase?"

"I found the hummer down Register Road, one wheel rim in the deep ditch, like you'd been run off the road. I couldn't find you and you didn't answer your cell. You can thank the sheriff for looking in the swamp. He figured that would be a good place to dump a…I mean, hide you."

I blinked.

"I'm just so glad the bastard didn't kill you."

I gulped and nodded.

"Logan, somebody wants you out of the picture. Do you have any idea who did this?"

I shook my head and moved the ice away from my lips. "I went to Acme Beavers' barn to check on Cy's horses. When I got back to the Hummer, I got punched."

"Are you thinking Acme?"

"I have no idea, really. Nobody was home. Not him, his wife, or kids. I guess anybody could have followed me there."

"You must be getting too close to finding out who killed Clara Banoak. Somebody's trying to stop you. Whoever did it took your weapons." Chase stood, limped over, and tried to find a spot to kiss me. "They gave you a sedative. I'm going to pull up this recliner and stay with you, but no more talking."

"You don't have to stay, Chase. I see you're still limping. You need rest yourself."

"I do have to stay. You're the most important thing in my life. I'm not leaving you." He kissed me again. "My ankle is fine, and I can keep it elevated in this chair."

I smiled and tried to reach for his hand, but mine turned to lead. I wanted to tell him I'd talked with Raina, and that I now knew he hadn't cheated on me, but my tongue seemed sewn to the bottom of my mouth, and my eyelashes interlaced against my will, plunging me into deep sleep.

I could barely focus on a furry light. No. Lots of tiny white lights. In the shape of a tree. My good eye brought the hospital Christmas tree in the hall into focus.

"Good morning." Chase planted a kiss on my lips. I felt it, so my lips had deflated somewhat. "I don't know how much true rest you got, but you snored some. You also hollered out a few times."

"What did I holler?"

"Nothing that made any sense. I think you were trying to get away from somebody or something."

"Probably the old night terrors I once had. They seem to show up when I'm traumatized. Did you sleep?"

"Enough. I kept my foot elevated all night. And I hope you don't mind, but I went through your phone contacts and called Pepper. She's already sent flowers." I turned my tender head toward the short chest of drawers beside me. The crystal vase, at least a foot tall, contained gorgeous flowers of every type and color.

"Wow! She likes to show off!" I beamed.

"She said she'd be in touch, and she loves you."

"I love her too. She's been a great friend."

"She has."

I shifted. "Chase?"

"Yeah?"

"I need to tell you something." He came closer. "But first, I need some ice or a sip of water."

He found the plastic water pitcher, and spooned an ice cube into my mouth.

"Um, that feels so good."

"It might help with the swelling too."

I swallowed and cleared my throat.

"Chase, I talked to Raina. I should have told you days ago."

"When did you talk to her?"

"You must have dropped your cell phone after Cy's funeral.

I heard it ringing and picked it up. I should have given it right back to you."

"I thought I'd lost it around the river somewhere. I'm glad to know you found it."

"Raina told me what happened. I'm sorry I didn't trust you, Chase. Please forgive me. I know how beautiful she is and that you two were an item before…"

"Long before you came into the picture, Logan. Raina's assertive, but she's not a bad girl. She needs to find a nice guy. She wants to be married, I think, and it doesn't matter to whom."

"I think you're wrong about that. She wants you. She said I was very lucky and to take good care of you or she would."

"You will, won't you?" He grinned.

"I did offer to loan you some panties, didn't I?" We both laughed.

"At least your memory seems to be coming back."

A knock at the door got our attention.

"Hey, Sheriff."

Gunn stepped in with a small vase of flowers.

"Agent Hunter, I can't say you look good, but you look better. I have everybody working on who did this to you. That deer stand's been in Hell Swamp for so long it's hard to remember who built the dang thing. I want to think it was Sly Foxx's daddy, but he's in a nursing home now. Sly said he didn't know either, and that wasn't their land, so anybody could have hauled you out there and left you.

"I'm trying to find out who owns that property. Once belonged to a Mathers, but I'm not sure it still does. We're checking some truck tracks, but there's not much to go on. We pulled your Hummer in and checked it over for prints. Somebody had to drive it into that ditch. Can you remember anything about where you were, or what you were doing when you were attacked?"

"Not much. I told Chase I'd checked on Cy's horses at Acme Beavers' barn and went back to the Hummer. I didn't think anybody was home. Oh, but Sheriff, you do need to go back to the swamp. While I was trying to walk out, I came across something awful."

"What's that?"

"A skull."

"Well, there's more than likely a ton of skulls out there, mostly deer, I'd expect."

"No. No, sir. This one was human."

"A human skull?" Chase showed interest. "Are you sure about that, Logan? You were pretty messed up out there."

"Yeah, I'm sure. That I remember even though most of it is fuzzy. It wasn't long before you found me."

"You're positive it wasn't a deer?"

I nodded at Gunn.

"We'll check it out. We have had a few missing persons over the years who never turned up." I remembered Cy telling me about people who disappeared in Hell Swamp.

"Anyways, back to the matter at hand," Gunn said. "I talked to Acme on his cell phone. He said his wife and children left for the week, visiting kin. He said he'd fed the horses and gone to Wilmington by himself. He didn't know of anybody who could be a witness to that though."

So Acme didn't have an alibi. This news made me restless, but I didn't know exactly why. Something niggling inside my brain needed to work its way out. I knew one thing for sure—

Christmas was coming, and I still had no idea who killed Clara Banoak or Cyrano Blood.

Once the hospital released me, Chase somehow got my Hummer, his Jeep, and me to Genesis Beach. He settled me on a couch by the window, found my pencil Christmas tree, and decorated it, putting a small present beneath it. He made sure I had everything I needed at arm's length before he headed west to appear for Raina's court date, with my blessing.

I stayed in bed the rest of the day and most of the next, but I didn't feel like I could waste any more time away from the crime scene. As soon as I felt like I could drive, I reached Chase on his cell and told him I was heading back. He said he'd meet me there with a travel trailer he'd borrowed from a friend in Asheville. That sounded good to me. At least we'd have somewhere to rest without a long drive to the beach every day.

I left the beach with the Hummer's window opened and took my time to make certain my vision was clear enough. The left eye still blurred some, but the right eye worked fine, so I had no problem driving. Dr. Eakins said it might take weeks for my vision to clear up completely, but I had no permanent damage to the cornea. I was lucky, and I knew it.

By the time I passed the crossroads near Canetuck and slowed for something dark moving in the road, I rolled up the window because I shivered from the cold air. With my good eye I could see several guinea hens looking for bugs in the high weeds along the edge of the road. If they weren't careful, they would be in somebody's stew pot by suppertime. The temperature dropped. I looked around at dark clouds gathering as I drove southwest.

I hadn't seen guineas in many years. I smiled. They exhumed another memory from childhood. We didn't have guineas, but a friend of my daddy's did, along with one conceited albino peacock. Daddy would occasionally take me to see these unusual birds. As I looked back at the guineas, I figured there must not be any dogs nearby to run them up.

Dog! I'd completely forgotten about Homer! Was he still tied up? Was he being fed? I floored the Hummer and screeched into Cy's yard a few miles farther, seeing a brown lump behind the house. I hopped out and ran to a weak hound. Somebody chained him back up, and he'd been fed, at least sporadically, but I didn't see any water source. I unchained him and he licked my face before trotting off to soak several trees. I found a container and filled it with water from the spigot on the back of Cy's house. Homer lapped for a minute, licked me, and then lapped some more. Then he took off at a run, sniffing the ground and baying.

"Homer! Come back!" I whistled, but he paid me no mind. I saw him run into the highway and take a left.

Where is he going?

I drove around looking for him, going back and forth down the paved road, and I turned off at a path near the river. No dog. I stopped and retrieved my heavy jacket from the back of the Hummer. As I did, snowflakes splattered on it and melted.

I sped back past the church with its large gravestones, and a thought occurred to me. I pulled into the cemetery and got out, bundling my coat around me. I saw his brown head lift as I approached. Homer's long body stretched out across Cy's grave with both front paws on the clay mound as he let out pitiful groans. I sat down beside the dog, and sobbed too. Sobbed over losing Cy. Sobbed over the botched-up murder case that seemed dead in the water. Sobbed over lost opportunities with Chase. I comforted Homer the best I could as snow fell on both of us and settled on the grave.

Eighteen

One day later I encountered Ethan Daw, driving Hawk's truck again. This time he had some other teenagers with him. I was glad to see him with kids his own age rather than Nita, who had to be closer to Hawk's age. He waved, and I waved back, noticing several more kids in the truck bed. They had poles, so I figured they were going fishing even though we had snow flurries the day before and it was quite cold.

In my rearview, I caught a glimpse of Ethan's strange friend, Lilith, her face still pale, her hair ink black, cowering down in the back of the truck. It had to be cold back there with the winter air and the truck's movement. The teenagers all wore heavy black coats with hoods, so I guessed they were prepared for the riverbank in winter.

I headed for the sheriff's office to see if any new evidence had surfaced in the Banoak case. I needn't have bothered. In Burgaw I stocked up on groceries and checked out a couple of local shops. I bought a sweatshirt and some warm socks since the camper might get nippy at night.

At dusk I drove back down the country road and caught a glimpse of a large fire over to my left by the river.

Those kids must have caught enough to have a fish fry.

I decided to pull in and meet Ethan's other friends. I didn't drive quietly but they were loud, having a wild time laughing and jumping around near the fire. I parked behind Hawk Daw's old farm truck, stepped out, and stopped in my tracks.

This was no fishing trip. All the teenagers dressed in black, even Ethan now. He had a black hood pulled over his head, but I recognized him because he was much taller than the others. The girls, Lilith and some blonde, dressed in black with net sleeves, engaged in ear-splitting shrieks, jumping near the fire as though they teased it, as though they wanted to jump in. The boys fanned the flames with their trench coats. I recognized the Goth look.

Cy found the remains of cats and dogs and evidence of a camp-fire near here. And isn't this where I found the torn black fabric?

I hadn't come here ready to hide and watch. I was out in the open, and it was just a matter of time before they saw me. I took the opportunity to observe as much as possible, although I wasn't certain I wanted to know about this. My stomach tightened as I watched them fanning the flames and hollering words I'd never heard before, much like the strange language I'd heard at Rose Paul's church. But there was something sinister and demonic about these words and the way they said them, the sounds being held in a thick cold mist near their mouths. My skin prickled, not from the night's chill, but from the realization that this was a cult, possibly a satanic cult. One of the boys was in the river, apparently sniggling—wrestling a catfish barehanded. I shifted my weight to get a better look, and Ethan spotted me and motioned for everyone in his party to get quiet.

"Agent Hunter, what are you doing here?" His tone was unpleasant and his speech tight, as though he chose his words carefully. He smoked a small cigar. Another surprise. But, really, I didn't know much about this kid at all. The others remained quiet and motionless, pulling their hoods closer around their faces to hide their identities.

"I drove by and saw the big fire. I thought I might get a fried fish over here." I tried to act innocent, but Ethan didn't appear to be buying it.

"We aren't fishing. We ate hot dogs." With that, he flipped his cigarillo into the fire.

"I thought maybe you were cat-fishing. I saw fishing poles in the back of your truck earlier today."

"No, they're not fishing poles, just poles." Ethan walked toward me in the darkness, his skin looking as pale as Lilith's, his eyes encircled with sinister-looking designs. His face didn't carry a pleasant look, and he certainly didn't look like a fifteen-year-old. Most of all, he didn't look innocent. I wasn't sure of his intentions, so I eased my long fingers around my new Glock.

As the tall young man approached me, my cell phone rang, startling both of us. He didn't take another step. I was relieved to hear Chase on the other end, telling me he would soon arrive with the camper.

"I'm sorry I intruded. I thought a fish fry would be fun, and I'd get to meet your friends officially. I'm sorry for interfering, Ethan. Gotta go."

I turned to leave, wondering where Hawk Daw and the other parents were, and if they had any idea what their children were up to.

"See you, Lilith!" I called out for good measure as I left. I didn't want to get into a confrontation with the three boys and two girls out in the boondocks. Not yet anyway. It was none of my business unless they were doing something illegal.

As I drove away, the predicted snow started again.

I didn't accomplish much before Chase pulled in with the camper. I was weak and sore, not to mention frustrated with the lack of trace evidence from the Banoak murder. Relentless gale-force winds drove a flurry of snow, but I didn't mind it so much. I'd had enough of heat and humidity. I sighed at beautiful swirls of flakes playing in the air. Even so, a gnawing deep within troubled me. Gnawing concern about why I'd been assaulted. Gnawing fear about what the teenagers had really been up to in the woods by the river. Gnawing guilt from this miserable excuse of an investigation.

I hung out inside the Banoak house for a while, trying to wrap my brain around some missing piece of information buried in my head, something I needed to remember for my own sake. The nerve in my damaged eye felt like a pinball in an arcade game. I figured my nerves, in general, were frayed, and by the time Chase arrived I sat under the Banoak shed, watching it snow and stroking Homer, who enjoyed his freedom to sniff around, and his new best friend, who would, undoubtedly, spoil him rotten.

Chase grinned and patted Homer while planting a kiss on my lips. "Ours?"

"I suppose so. Nobody took care of him. I just couldn't leave him there."

"Maybe ole Homer will come in handy." He patted a willing head while Homer reciprocated with a lick.

Chase got permission from one of Clara's neighbors to set up the camper across the highway from the house, along the edge of a wide dirt road, so his Jeep would be free to drive.

The trailer door opened to the sleeper/sofa on the right, miniature kitchen on the left, and dining area for four people, which turned into a bed. I couldn't say much for the colors, but what did that matter anyway? The trailer would shelter us and save us exhausting drives back to the beach. I stepped up and walked to the double bed that took up the entire room when opened, and peeked into the bathroom, large enough for a shower, sink, and commode. It would do.

We could both sleep here without being carted off by Teeth. We could sleep separately or together. We could cook some decent food instead of having to eat stale sandwiches brought in and kept past their expiration dates, picked up at Yonder Store or some gas station. Chase brought a small generator so we could have heat. Not much room for a large basset hound, though, so we'd probably have to leave Homer outside.

I drove Chase's Jeep and he and Homer rode with me back to the beach to pick up a few items of clothing and comfort for the camper. Chase was unusually quiet. Tired, I figured, from the twelve-hour trip to and from Asheville. Homer enjoyed having his ears flap in the breeze. Even though it was cold, we obliged him. We would have had the top down if we could have, since Homer manufactured lethal farts.

"What on earth have you been feeding him?" Chase groaned.

"Not much yet. But somebody had been feeding him some occasional table scraps, I think. He's probably eaten anything he could find since I unchained him."

We gave the dog a few minutes to run the beach and expel the rest of his pent-up flatulence while I grabbed a few pots and pans, some staples from the kitchen cabinets, and several bottles of Duplin's Christmas wine and two flutes. I looked around at Chase, who gathered a part of my Santa collection to take to the camper.

"What? I love Christmas!" I just grinned and shook my head. He ignored me and packed them anyway.

We stopped and bought a few other groceries including a fifty-pound bag of dog food and a couple of steaks since Chase had found a small grill in the trailer's storage area.

Back at Black River, I put sheets on the double bed and nuked some potatoes while Chase started the charcoal and salad. I'd brought along another set of linens for the sofa, even though I'd leave that decision to Chase. We enjoyed the evening, listening to the river's nightlife from a safe distance with our bellies satisfied. Chase got out the Santas and set them on the windowsill behind the sink.

"Are you happy now?"

"No, Logan, I'm not." He turned to face me. "This'll be my mother's last Christmas."

"What do you mean?"

I'd met Fern Railey, and she seemed in great health and lived a pampered lifestyle in Asheville. But Chase's father, a prominent attorney, had been arrested and convicted of financing the operation of several huge meth labs and raking in millions of dollars from market-ready marijuana. So she had probably had a few setbacks of various kinds.

"What's happened?"

"Cancer. It's in her brain, Logan. She's dealing with it, but she looks terrible. I knew her voice sounded odd the last few times I've talked to her, but I didn't expect this. She wanted to tell me in person. My going back for court gave her the opportunity."

"Is she on chemo? Can't something be done?"

"She refused any treatment. She said she'd been to three of the best doctors in the state, including one at Duke. They all told her to get her final arrangements in order."

"I'm so sorry, Chase." I hugged him for a few seconds and then he pulled away.

"Dad did this to her." I wanted to say something, but I wasn't sure what was appropriate. I'd met his father, Drew Railey, a despicable man. While I didn't know if he could cause cancer, I did know he'd caused a lot of grief, embarrassment, and hurt, not only for his wife but also for his only son.

"Who'll take care of her, Chase?"

"Clive. Remember him?"

"The English butler? Sure. I liked him."

"Well, I've thought for a long time that he loves Mother, so he won't abandon her. In fact, she confided in me that she plans to leave him a significant amount of compensation for looking after her all these years. She asked if I minded. I told her I didn't."

"I'm glad Fern has him there." I got quiet and snuggled with Chase, which he seemed to appreciate. Snow barely covered the ground, but it silenced most critters for the night. We took showers and rubbed cream on each other's insect bites. Then he covered my bruises with Vitamin E, but we were content to cuddle without going any farther.

A hard knock on the door early the next morning jarred the

little camper and us. Homer, who managed to win us over and stay inside, barked nonstop. Chase scrambled to the door, pulling on his jeans. He apparently didn't recognize the man looking up at him.

"Mister, is Agent Hunter in there?"

"Who wants to know?"

I scrambled into some clothes of my own.

"Ezra Overpeck. I'm Cyrano Blood's cousin. I came to get the hawses, but listen, I gotta see her right now! I'm all to pieces." I stuck my head around Chase, noticing how rattled the man appeared and how his body shook.

"What's wrong, Mr. Overpeck?"

"You gotta come, Agent Hunter. To the barn where the hawses are. I just can't tell you. You have to see it for yourself."

We told him we'd follow him. We snatched the keys and barreled down the road while I held my woozy head.

"You okay?"

"I'm trying to remember. Something happened between the time I checked on the horses and when I was attacked. Something I saw. I just can't bring it back."

"Maybe Mr. Overpeck saw the same thing."

We ran to Acme's barn. Mr. Overpeck pointed to the loft but refused to go back into the barn. He stayed outside with his hands rammed down into his deep pockets while we ran to the ladder.

Chase climbed up and jerked backwards. "Call the sheriff, Logan!" His face blanched.

I dialed Gunn and asked him to come to Acme's property immediately, took a long gulp of air, and climbed up to the loft to look.

"Chase! This is what I couldn't remember. I saw these…these things, ran to the Hummer, and got hit before I could call anyone."

I planted my foot on the loft floor and pulled myself up. I inched my way around the rotting card table, getting as close as

I dared to the two decayed corpses.

The woman had a few strands of very long stringy hair, filled with dust and cobwebs, and an unusually long face with a square chin. The eyes were long gone, and no flesh remained around her nostrils. Her unhinged mouth revealed some missing teeth. She wore the remnants of a dress in what might have been pale pink lace at one time. Chase tossed me his digital camera, and I began to take one frightful picture after another.

I moved to the man wearing a rotten tuxedo. Stringy hair hung down to his clavicle, loaded with dust and cobwebs. No flesh attached to his nose or mouth, eyes rolled back to reveal only the dusty whites. Both corpses appeared to be just shy of losing their heads.

"I'd say Acme Beavers has a lot of explaining to do."

Chase checked the house where I'd first visited the Beavers family. Nobody.

From the loft, I watched Ogden Gunn and two deputies speed up and jump out of their cars.

"Whatcha got?"

Chase pointed for Gunn to look for himself. He pulled his body up the ladder and peered over the edge of the loft. "Geez-shit! Acme. I'd never have believed it." Gunn shook his head from side to side as he descended. I followed him.

To his deputies, Gunn snapped, "You boys get up there and see if you can identify them people. And don't touch nothing. I'm calling Lemmie." He turned to us. "Acme has a license in taxidermy. Did you know that?" We shook our heads. "He told us his parents died in a wreck, but if that turns out to be his family up there, he's in hawg shit up to his hairy eyebrows."

He spit out a toothpick and headed for his cruiser while the deputies covered their faces with handkerchiefs and eased up the ladder.

Lemmie arrived and identified the two sets of remains as Acme's mother and father. "I'm sure of it, but I'll check dental records anyway." He stood up straight and looked at me. "What does all this mean, Agent Hunter? Why would Acme do such a thing?"

"Because they didn't die in a car wreck off somewheres like he's always said, Lemmie. He killed 'em and stuffed 'em," Gunn said.

"Wait, now. Just wait a minute," I said. "We don't know Acme did it, although he's the most logical possibility. But I need to find out where he is now. He and his family."

"Is he the one who attacked you?" added Chase. "And if he did, why?"

I had no idea.

Nineteen

The sheriff had a few ideas.

"It seems like Acme went to a shrink for awhile, but Dr. Brown won't give out any information. All's I know is Acme got a license in taxidermy and took care of most of the hunters around here, but it didn't last that long. He lost interest and started turning people away. This was after he went to work at the pulpwood plant in Delco.

"Then he said he'd just do taxidermy as a hobby and only then for big bucks. Most everybody was some kind of disappointed because they had to drive all the way to Burgaw or Wilmington after that to find a taxidermist."

"Did he lose interest about the time his parents were in the wreck?"

The sheriff lifted his hat and replaced it. "Come to think of it, yes. It was about that time, I'm just about certain."

"After what we found, I'm worried about his wife and children. Where could they be? And where's Acme? We need to contact the plant, and any family members to see if they went on vacation, or just disappeared."

Gunn's face paled. "You're not suggesting Acme killed them, are you?"

"I don't know what to think, Sheriff. Let's not jump to conclusions just yet."

"What school do his kids attend?" Chase had his pad out. "I'll see if they're in school."

"Good idea. They'd both be at the middle school near Burgaw. Hold on. I'll get the phone number," Gunn said. He fumbled around in the cruiser and came out with a shabby phone book. He thumbed through and parked his index finger on a line, spouting out the numbers as Chase dialed.

"Well, neither of them are in school," Chase told us once the secretary checked attendance. "But she said it was nothing new; they miss about two out of five days a week."

"Why does that not surprise me?"

Chase went house to house, asking if anyone had seen the Beavers family. Homer and I went over Acme's house and yard with renewed determination. I picked up anything that looked out of place, and Homer seemed content to sniff and pee all over the yard. He didn't miss a tree. I had to take the time to call in for another evidence-collection kit. I'd used up all my bags and containers and sent them to the lab.

I searched behind the Beavers house, looking at a suspicious rag. I heard a noise and turned to see an old man watching me from behind a tree. Homer and I walked in his direction as he retreated quickly, considering he was barefooted and had the walking farts.

"Hey!"

He kept going. I extended my gun and pulled the trigger, dropping a limb directly in his path.

"What thuh hell?"

I grabbed the backs of his arms and spun him around as he wobbled to the ground. He threw both hands up when he saw the gun.

"Who are you?"

"Huh?"

"WHO ARE YOU?"

"Leak. Dick Leak." *I've been told about this busybody.*

"What are you doing here?"

"What? I can't hear."

No freaking kidding.

"WHAT ARE YOU DOING HERE?"

"Nothing, really."

He looked suspicious.

"THIS IS A CRIME SCENE. YOU SHOULDN'T BE HERE."

"Yeah, there's some bees here. Over in that tree yonder," he said, pointing. "You looking for honey?"

Oh, for Pete's sake!

Homer sniffed the man's nasty crotch like it was rotten meat and slobbered all over his pants leg before I helped him up.

"Tell me why you're on Acme Beavers' property."

"What?"

"TELL ME WHY YOU'RE ON BEAVERS' PROPERTY!"

"We're neighbors is all. I walk over here a lot of the time."

"YOU SEE THIS YELLOW CRIME TAPE?" He nodded. "IT CLEARLY WARNS PEOPLE TO STAY OUT."

"I…I didn't mean to upset your apple cart, ma'am."

With growing impatience, I said, "Look, Mr. Leak," I touched his shoulder, "YOU'VE GOT TO LEAVE THE PREMISES."

He nodded again.

"BUT, SIR, DO YOU HAVE A CLEAN CONTAINER I CAN BORROW?"

"You're an entertainer?" He smiled until Homer forcefully stuck his nose into the man's crotch, deeper this time. That dog had some nerve.

"NO! NO, I NEED A CONTAINER! A BUCKET, BOX, LARGE CAN."

"You can do the can-can? I'll be! I thought for a minute that was a real gun. It looks real."

I grabbed him with one hand and found my badge with the gunned hand.

"That fake too?"

"NO, IT'S REAL, Piss Teeth!" I shoved the gun to his temple and made a menacing face at him, already frustrated at how many hours I would lose trying to interrogate this idiot.

Homer began to growl and show teeth. I reached to pat his head since I didn't want the man to lose his testicles right in front of me.

Well, maybe one.

Dick Leak nodded his head, almost grinning. "You're good. You look real mean."

Just as I released him I heard a noise behind me. I spun with my gun ready. Homer jerked around and let out a series of loud, deep barks, directed at the latest stranger on the scene.

"Excuse me, Agent Hunter?" A young black man with protruding ears approached, displaying his SBI badge from a distance. "I'm Agent Rice. Lamar Rice. Kent Poletti assigned me to assist you in any way I can."

"DON'T MOVE," I directed to Dick Leak. I turned back to Rice. "Poletti hasn't called me. He always calls ahead."

"Maybe you could check your voicemail? I know he tried." The man showed me his official badge from a closer position.

I did as he suggested, and sure enough, I had two messages from Poletti to expect Agent Rice.

"Agent Rice, this is Mr. Leak. Richard Leak. I was about to question him about the murders of Clara Banoak and Cyrano Blood. Mr. Leak, it seems, is a snoop. He sees a lot. He probably knows a lot. The problem is he doesn't hear well. I'm turning him over to you. I assume you've been briefed?"

He nodded.

"Okay. Get all the information you can about any and everything he's seen. Oh, and talk loud." I started to walk away. "I've got to find an uncontaminated container to put some possible evidence in."

"I have a kit. Get what you need from the trunk of the sedan. I'll call in for another one." I thanked him and headed for the old dark blue headquarters-issued car.

I heard Agent Rice begin. "Mr. Leak?"

"No, I don't need to piss. I took one behind that tree yonder a while ago."

I snickered even though we needed to know what that man might have seen, touched, or carted off.

"MR. LEAK?"

"Yeah."

"I'm Agent Rice. I need to ask you some questions while Agent Hunter searches the yard."

"Did you know that woman's an entertainer?"

"What? NO, MR. LEAK. SHE'S AN SBI AGENT."

"Really? A real one?"

"YES, SIR."

"And that gun was real?"

"YEP!"

"I'll be damn!"

I called to Homer, and we moved around the yard. I was glad to have relieved myself of dealing with Dick Leak, who might not only be deaf, but also a barefooted fruitcake with brown teeth. It was far too cold to be going without shoes.

I scoured the yard and entered the unlocked house, a pigsty compared to Cyrano's. Apparently Rachel Blanche and the children left in a hurry. I put on some gloves and picked through the mess, looking for any clue that might help solve the two murders.

"This place is a Dumpster!"

I whirled around. "MR.LEAK! WHAT ARE YOU DOING IN HERE?"

"Huh?"

"PUT THAT DOWN! DON'T TOUCH ANOTHER DAMN THING!" He held a rechargeable phone that he'd evidently found on the floor under some papers.

"YOU COULD BE DESTROYING EVIDENCE, YOU SON OF A BITCH!"

Agent Rice appeared in the doorway, looking embarrassed.

"Sorry, Agent Hunter. I had to make a phone call, and he slipped away from me."

I beat the sides of my legs. Hard. I wanted to put my fist

through this man's scrawny face. But really, what the hell difference did it make? Everything about these cases, all the evidence, had somehow been mucked up.

"RICHARD LEAK, YOU'RE UNDER ARREST FOR OB-STRUCTING JUSTICE," I bellowed at him. That got his attention.

I pointed my gun at Leak, deciding whether to shoot his freaking head off or let Homer have his nuts for a snack, as Chase came in.

"What's going on?"

"This moron is tampering with the crime scene and possible evidence."

"I'm sure it's tempting to shoot him," Chase declared.

"You have no idea."

"But, Logan, don't do it."

Leak wandered over to Chase. "Who're you? Another agent?"

"YEAH, THAT'S RIGHT." Chase hollered in the deaf man's face, "but you don't have to worry about me. THAT WOMAN OVER THERE'S YOUR WORST NIGHTMARE. SHE'S READY TO BLOW YOUR HEAD OFF. I ADVISE YOU TO STAY OUT OF HER WAY."

The man lurched for the door, looking pale, and I hoped, ready to get the hell out of the way, so I didn't arrest him. Not yet anyway.

Just to make sure he got out of our way, Chase, Homer, and I escorted him to his house through a grove of overgrown trees and vines. He'd worn a path, so it appeared he'd been spying on Acme and his family for some time. In fact, several well-worn paths led off in different directions from Leak's porch.

Who else had he spied on? Maybe Cy? I felt like punching his scrawny ass.

Leak's house, a small cabin with a pointed roof way oversized for the cabin, looked new and like one of the kits you can order. It sat on a thin slab of concrete with no other foundation.

A window air conditioner had been fitted into a cutout below the double window. Some unpainted latticework marked the entry to the front door. A stovepipe jutted up from near the front roof corner. A flowered flag swayed in the breeze on the other side of the cabin. No grass or shrubbery. Not far away in the other direction another well-worn path passed a spent vegetable garden and continued all the way to the side of Cyrano Blood's house at least a half mile away.

"DID YOU SPY ON CYRANO?"

"No, that there path belongs to me! It's on my property." He sat down on a stump under a tree while chickens ran around and pecked at the ground near him and down the path. He seemed to be as tired of us as we were of him, so Chase and I headed back to Acme's house, hollering for Homer to come along. He peed on everything he could cock his leg on. I had to laugh at him, and I wasn't going to stop him if he pissed all over Leak.

The sheriff, who had been called back to his office, returned to the scene and caught up with us. He said he had some new information I might be interested in.

"What's that?"

"The Phillip Mathers estate still owns the swamp you were in."

"Why would anybody buy a swamp?"

"It hasn't always been wet there. Years ago there was a bad flood, and the river crested many feet above the banks. Water collected in every low place around here. No way to get it out. Anyways, Mathers has been dead since 1979, but that skull you mentioned?"

"Yes?"

"It could belong to his grandson, who ran away when he was about fifteen. He never came back, and nobody ever heard hide nor hair of him again. Some say he was a little touched in the head. We're looking for the rest of him, but I doubt we'll find anything. Draining that swamp would be dang near impossible. I'm sending the skull to Raleigh."

I supposed that answered two questions, but we still had to find the Beavers family. Nobody had seen them in a while, so Chase, Homer, and I rode to Delco to corner and question Acme. We needn't have bothered. The manager of the plant said Acme had taken leave for a "personal emergency."

We split up and questioned a few people on the same shift Acme worked, but nobody could tell us any more than the supervisor had. The Beavers children had still not reported or called in to school. The disarray of their house made this news even more distressing.

We stopped at Yonder Store on the way back to the camper and caught Sly Foxx coming out. He suggested we ask Nita about Acme's whereabouts.

"Nita?"

"Sure. Acme was her first husband. They were married for over ten years. She ought to know where his family lives."

"Chase, how could I have forgotten that? I'm going to Quicki Realty in Wilmington. Why don't you find Agent Rice and get acquainted? And monitor Leak. He's a busybody. He'll be around. I wonder how many things he's touched or moved from Acme's and Cy's—and maybe even Clara's."

The house-turned-office on Wrightsville Avenue near Bradley Creek, composed of two rooms and a bathroom, was unexpectedly tiny. The waiting room was stunning, in lemony yellow with white furniture, yellow gingham drapes, and white antique end tables, each with a vase of realistic flowers in acrylic. A gorgeous Christmas tree sat in the corner on an oak floor. It was more like home than a realtor's office, more than likely the point.

A gray-haired man stuck his head around the corner from the other room. I could see an untidy desk. "Can I help you?"

"I'm here to see Ms. Quicki," I stated, showing my badge.

"SBI." He reached for his thick hair and patted it.

"Is anything wrong, sir?"

"It's just that Nita's on the phone with a customer from out-of-state who wants to buy a house here. She'll be a few minutes. I'm sorry you have to wait. Please take a seat."

He motioned me to an upholstered chair.

"This has been very difficult for Nita. Oh, I haven't introduced myself. I'm Marvin Quicki." We shook hands. "We own the realty together."

"I remember her telling me she owned it with her husband."

"Ex," he answered, almost in a whisper. He looked as though he wanted to say more, but stopped himself as Nita appeared in the doorway.

"Marvin, I'll take it from here." He disappeared around the corner like a scolded dog.

Nita showed me into her office, decorated with a few holiday touches.

"I like your office. It's very welcoming."

"Thanks. I want my customers to relax and tell me exactly what they're looking for. I think the dining table and chairs make them feel more at ease." This room, painted the same yellow, featured a small dining table with a three-light chandelier above, a built-in china cabinet filled with neatly stacked papers, white blinds on a sunny window, and an antiqued sideboard with a large mirror. A white table-high counter with cabinets and drawers provided a place for Nita's laptop and paperwork. A white corkboard loaded with pictures of homes hung above it.

"I really didn't do much. It was maid's quarters and belonged with the huge house right behind it, but I wanted it. I just took out a few things and turned it into a reception area and dining room, a.k.a. office. Marvin hangs out in what was once a closet. He likes it, and it keeps his mess out of mine."

"Nita, I've just remembered you were married to Acme Beavers at one time." She closed the door.

"Marvin gets upset about my other husbands," she said, loud enough for him to hear on the other side of the door. "Yes. Why? What's going on with Acme? Surely you don't think he killed Mama?"

"I'm sure you heard about Cyrano Blood. We need to question Acme about that. Do you know where we can reach him?"

"I reckon he'd be at work. How should I know?" She moved to the counter and lit a cigarette. Her face flushed and her tone of voice became cold and less friendly.

"He's not at work. Do you know where he might be? Where he's from? Where his family or his wife's relatives live? And I need his cell phone number."

"Acme doesn't have a cell phone. Neither does Rachel Blanche."

"That's odd. Sheriff Gunn said he'd talked to Acme on a cell phone earlier."

"Well, if he has one, he hasn't given me the number."

She was lying, but I let it go. I'd get Acme's number from Gunn.

She blew smoke at me. "Acme's from Saxapahaw, on the other side of Durham. It'll take you a couple of hours from here, maybe more. I don't know why he'd go there, since his parents are dead. His wife's from Toast. Maybe they went there."

"Toast?" I continued to be amazed at how many little towns in North Carolina I'd never heard of.

"Just head west on Interstate 40 to Winston-Salem, then turn north on 421. That's all I know."

"Have you ever been to Toast?"

"No, but I've been to Saxapahaw. I've heard him talk about Toast though. Rachel Blanche, Acme's wife, talks very little."

"What's her maiden name?"

"Uhmm, Berryhill, I think. Yeah, Rachel Blanche Berryhill."

"About your business partner…"

"Marvin?"

"Yes. He's your last husband. Is that correct?"

"Yes, Agent Hunter. My last name's Quicki."

"And you two are divorced."

"Correct again. Why?"

"Just curious. You mentioned he gets upset about your other husbands. I assume he knew about them before he married you."

Nita gave me a sideways glance. "Most of them, yeah. So?"

"He obviously still has feelings for you."

"I guess so." She walked over toward the door in a haughty manner. "But then, all of my exes still have feelings for me." She opened the door and gestured me out.

Yeah, but what kinds of feelings? Love? Hate? Animosity? Could poor old Marvin still love her enough to kill her mother in hopes of winning her back?

I admit I wanted to go after Nita with all my guns. I still felt that she had killed her mother or hired her killed. I could feel it in my bones.

I needed motive. *For money? Because Clara knew something she shouldn't? Just for meanness?*

Twenty

I thought virtually everybody had a cell phone, but I was wrong. We had no contact number for Rachel Blanche Beavers or any of her relatives. We acquired Acme's cell number from Gunn, but he wasn't answering or hadn't charged up. This meant another long trip for us.

Chase drove his Jeep since Acme knew my Hummer and it used less gas. It took over four and one-half hours to get to Toast since we had to detour for Homer, who had apparently never ridden on such curvy roads. He got sick in the back seat and we pulled into a station near Mount Airy and hosed out the entire back of the Jeep and washed down the sides. I felt more sorry for the big pooch than I did for us. We were all stuck for the duration, although once he'd emptied, we didn't give Homer a single bite of anything for the remainder of the trip.

Toast was a hilly farming community, the scenery still spectacular even though the fall colors were disappearing. The pond we approached displayed plenty of turtles, sunning themselves on logs or debris strong enough to hold them. Beautiful shrubs of some sort, in hot pink, bloomed near the road. We pulled over to stretch our legs and give Homer a chance to put four paws on terra firma, just to avoid another bout of motion sickness.

Chase and I sat by the pond, wrapped in a blanket I'd dug out from under his seat, and ate fresh toasted subs and chips we bought at the last stop. I watched as an old red work truck crept up the mountainside between rows of Christmas trees that would be cut and loaded on it before it eased its way back down. Each tree would be wrapped in netting and shipped to stores all over the country. I'd read somewhere that several North Carolina Christmas trees had been selected for presidents at the White House. North Carolina is, after all, the second largest Christmas tree-producing state in the country.

The tree plots, turned this way and that, created a panoramic quilt of plush green knots, a delight for my eyes. I felt the chill as the predicted cold front came over the mountains in the west, brushed my skin, and swept on toward the east coast.

The temperature dropped from a pleasant sixty degrees to a chilly forty degrees in no time. Chase and I nuzzled for a moment or two before Homer realized he might be missing out on something and tried to join us. It was time to go anyway, so we hopped up and loaded Homer into the Jeep to complete our drive to find the Beavers family.

Chase pulled into a Toast gas station and asked for directions to the Berryhills. The station attendant knew Mr. Berryhill and gave directions out to the farm, some fifteen miles farther. We drove through the downtown, a scenic, historic, quiet town, past the painted gazebo near the town hall, and turned right on Main Street. We turned off on a country road and passed pastures of cows, goats, and horses. Homer, who seemed to be over his motion sickness, barked at them off and on.

"Slow down. I think we're getting close," I said, pointing to a white farmhouse at least three hundred yards off the road. The mailbox confirmed that we entered Berryhill property. We drove up as Acme's children came running out of the house. They stopped in their tracks as Chase shut off the engine. We stepped out, and I asked if their parents were here.

"Mama is. Daddy ain't," said the buck-toothed boy.

We walked to the door as Rachel Blanche Berryhill Beavers pushed the screen door for us. "I knowed something terrible would happen," she said, fighting back tears. She wore a dress several sizes too large for her and had a dirty face and hands. "I've been pullin' collards and turnips. They're sweeter after the frost hits 'em, you know. Come on out back. My sister had to give me clothes 'cause we left with nothin'."

She turned toward the children. "You two stay away from that Jeep, now, ya hear?" They laughed and ran past it down the path we'd come in on, Homer chasing after them.

"Mrs. Beavers, we're looking for Acme. We have some questions for him."

"Yeah, I bet you do. I knowed he punched you, Miss. I saw him. I pitched a fit, and he told me to shut up and git to the house with the children." She spit out a disgusting plug of tobacco on the ground through her brown teeth.

"You witnessed that?"

"Oh yeah. We'd just come up from the field, and he saw you in the barn. It made him mad as a rattler. He don't like nobody messing out there. When you ran to your truck, he was waitin' for ya. I don't know why he did something like that. He goes off on a conniption fit ever now and then. I'm sorry you got hurt."

"Thank you. I'm glad to have that part of the mystery solved. Now, can you tell us where he is?"

"I know Acme had bad things in that barn. He threatened to kill the children and me if we ever went up the ladder. I never did, and I don't want you telling me neither."

Chase gave it a try. "Mrs. Beavers, where's your husband?" She stared at him as though we had never asked the question before.

"Why don't you ask Nita?"

"Nita? What's she got to do with this?"

"Nita was Acme's first wife."

"Yes, we know that, but…"

"He ain't never got over her. She pulls him back in ever time she wants something, and he'd do anything she said just to get into her slut britches."

Even kill her mother? Chase and I made eye contact, both re-alizing we'd been on a wild goose chase.

The trip to Toast had given me a witness to my assault, but little else. We sped to the interstate, set the cruise control on eighty-five and headed to Wilmington. I dialed Lamar Rice, sup-posed to be heading back to Raleigh by now, but with any luck, I might be able to divert him.

"Rice?"

"Agent Hunter?

"Can you detour?"

"I guess so. Where?"

"Wilmington." I gave him Nita Quicki's address and a de-scription of both Nita and Acme.

He said he'd find her and stake her out until we arrived. "I'm off the clock. You're lucky I haven't gone far. Poletti doesn't ex-pect me back for a couple of days, so I can help you for a little while."

"I appreciate it a lot, Agent Rice. Agent Railey and I are up to our eyeballs in this case. We suspect she's 'in concert with' a murderer. We're trying to corral him now. Then I want to talk to both of them."

"You want me to bring her in?"

"No, not yet. We think he'll go to her, or she'll find a way to get to him. That'll confirm some things. Don't let her spot you."

"I'll take care of it, ma'am." I smiled and pushed *Off.* I liked Agent Lamar Rice's manners. Only a couple of years older than he was, I liked the superior feeling 'ma'am' gave me.

We didn't slow down until the Quicki Realty office came into view, dark and locked up for the night. Not sure where Nita lived, we didn't intend to leave Wilmington until we'd been there. I dialed Rice but got no answer. Chase ran to a phone booth and looked up the Quicki Realty number for nighttime, a different address and phone number.

I checked on Homer in the backseat, looking sick again. We

had to stop taking him everywhere. He wasn't accustomed to so much traveling at a high rate of speed for hours, but this time none of us had a choice.

We turned left off Market Street onto Clay Hills Drive and found the house number on the wraparound porch, lit for easy reading. Rice had positioned his sedan across the street. He nodded as I walked to the front door with my finger on my gun while Chase went around some hedges to the back, in case Acme tried to run. I rang the bell, and Nita didn't seem surprised to see me when she opened the door.

"I heard about the barn."

"Is he here, Nita?"

"No."

"I don't believe you. Mind if I have a look around?" I pushed by her.

"Aren't you supposed to have a search warrant?"

"Yeah, I can get one. It'll take some time, but I can get one. In the mean time, Chase and I will make ourselves comfortable. I'll even go with you to pee, but we're not leaving without some information."

She looked at the back of the house where Chase stood in the doorway, and sighed.

"He isn't here. You're wasting your time and mine. Look all you want. He's gone."

"So he has been here."

"Yeah. He always runs to me when he's in trouble. He has no balls. No balls at all."

"You sent us on an all-day wild goose chase half way across the state for nothing. I believe we could call that obstruction of justice."

I sat with her while Chase went over the entire house. He found nothing.

"How long has he been gone?"

"Since about seven o'clock." *Three hours ago.*

"Where was he going?"

"Do I look like a psychic?" Nita, more agitated than I'd ever seen her, had a hateful tone.

"His wife says he spends more time with you than he does with her. You should know where he'd go."

"Good ole Rachel Blanche. She took the kids and ran, didn't she? I'm not surprised. She let herself go years ago, not that she was ever pretty. I never knew what Acme saw in her." Her tone softened a bit. "Look, I'm sorry I've deceived you, but there's something you ought to know about Acme. He has some serious problems."

Chase smirked at her. "No frickin' kidding!"

"I mean mental problems."

"Again, we're not surprised," Chase said.

"Nita," I said, "did you know Acme's parents were in the top of that old barn?"

She squirmed and looked down. "Yeah." She stood up and folded her arms over her chest. "I know, I know. But he made it into a loving tribute to them."

"A tribute? To let his parents decay in the elements? Loving is hardly the word for it."

"No, listen, you have to understand how Acme was. Is. He wrote poems to them. Tender, kind-hearted poems. Then he'd go up there and read them to his folks. He'd change their positions for a while, until it became too difficult, and dust off their clothes and get the cobwebs out of their hair. He loved them dearly."

"Then why did he kill them?"

"He didn't. He had them embalmed somewhere after the wreck and told the funeral home the family wanted to do the rest, a private funeral and burial in the Beavers cemetery. The funeral home didn't give him a hard time about it. I'm sure he paid them something. He could have embalmed them himself, I suppose, but they were already at a morgue when he found out about the wreck. Anyway, he dressed them and put them up there so he could visit them every day. It was off limits to everybody else. He didn't even allow Rachel Blanche and the children up there."

"Nita, you have to know how sick that is," I said in a soft voice.

"Acme was intensely sad and lonely. Nothing made him happy after they died. I tried my best. He'd sleep a lot, like he was drugged, but he wasn't. He'd tell me he couldn't feel anything at all. I took him to a therapist back when I thought I could help him. They diagnosed him with hypomania, but he never told the doctors about the barn. He seemed to be more comfortable with dead people than with living people. He could will himself to become numb and not feel a thing. A while after that he got a zoonosis. That didn't help matters any."

"I've read enough about hypomania to know it means he's a psychopath."

Chase interrupted. "And what's zoonosis?" We both looked to Nita for the answer to that one.

"It's an infectious disease you get from animals. Since Acme did taxidermy for a number of years, he contracted it that way, I suppose. I don't know that much about it, but I think it's kin to Mad Cow, Bird Flu, and Lyme Disease. It was serious. He had fever, myalgia, and respiratory problems. He was in the hospital for several weeks. He could have died. The hospital monitoring saved him. After that episode, I told him we were through. I'd had enough."

"Yet you're still involved," I said.

"Yep, up to your ass," Chase added. Nita just stared back at us, her face pale.

Maybe she'll give him up now.

"Nita, you've got to help us find him. Where would he go?"

"I can't imagine him being far away from his folks." Chase and I looked at each other and headed for the door.

We knew the corpses had been removed, but maybe Acme didn't know and was still in the area. To be sure we had a head start, Chase and I took Nita's cell phone and house phone so she couldn't contact him without getting in her car and driving to a phone booth. That way, at least we'd have a few minutes head start.

I asked Rice to continue surveillance of Nita and told him we'd head back to Black River. I felt somewhat guilty about not checking with Poletti, but the feeling didn't last long.

Twenty-One

After unloading a grateful Homer and switching the empty Jeep for the Hummer, Chase and I parked behind some thick bushes not too far from Acme's barn and eased around with our guns drawn. We searched the barn, but already expected it to be empty, law enforcement and Lemmie long gone with the skeletal remains we'd found earlier.

We heard a truck start up and ran around the bushes to watch Acme speed away. He had apparently hidden his truck from view and had been in the vicinity the whole time. He knew all the ins and outs of the river and the woods. Even though I felt like I'd been on the case forever, I knew where few paths led.

We pursued him to where the road forked at Yonder Store, and nearly caught up with him as he passed Singed Pig Road. He gunned the old truck, managing to keep it between the ditches past Gum Flat Road. He ducked unexpectedly down another road with Chase and me right behind him. Acme lost control when he approached Long Branch and the old pickup sailed off into it.

Chase ran to the driver's door and yanked Acme out, getting punched in the face before I got my gun's laser on Acme. It was dark as three feet up a bear's butt in the thick woods surrounding us, and Acme dissolved into the night.

Chase got his bearings, plugged in his searchlight, and combed the woods. He held the light as I maneuvered along the edge of the woods until we were back at the main highway. We called for backup, and Gunn, who'd developed gout in his big toe, said he'd send Deputy Horrell.

Chase, the deputy, and I spent hours searching, but decided the three of us couldn't find a man in his home territory, deep in the woods, on a moonless night. We called for more backup from surrounding counties, and staked out all four sides of the woods, knowing, even then, we couldn't cover thousands of acres.

Chase and I pulled down a dirt path that log trucks used to haul away cut timber. My head throbbed and the muscle around my damaged eye twitched uncontrollably. I pushed the seat back and dozed. Chase took the first shift and drank a bottle of water and ate a rice cake, the only food we had with us. I decided to do without.

I woke to find Chase's face practically in mine, his eyes closed. I sighed. We weren't doing a good job of staking out the woods. I sat up and nudged him awake.

"This is pointless. Let's go back to the camper and get some rest. Acme could have walked up and blown our brains out while we slept in the Hummer. He'll show up again."

"I don't know, Logan. Why would he stay around now that the bodies...um, skeletal remains, are gone?"

Chase had a point. We'd made a mistake. We should have left the remains alone until we apprehended Acme. Now that he knew they'd been removed, and Rachel Blanche and the children had left, he had no reason to come back.

"I smell smoke!" That smell got stronger as I saw flames. "We've got to get out of here!"

"Yep, I do believe the woods are on fire," Chase said. "You think Acme would set a fire to trap us in?"

"You bet your sweet ass he would."

I gunned the Hummer, both sides of the path now ablaze. Ahead of me flames crossed the narrow path. Chase tried to get someone on the radio, but he only got static.

"It's a straight shot, Logan."

I put the accelerator to the floor and we held on and plowed through the inferno, having no idea if we'd come out on the other side. The Hummer's metal was hot, but I kept both hands on the steering wheel and held my breath for as long as I could. Chase coughed uncontrollably.

The fire leapt at us on both sides, in front, and now behind us. I tried to mash the gas pedal farther down, but it was already down as far as it could go. My eyes burned and teared from the smoke and heat—and the very real possibility that Chase and I might have it all end here, in Hell.

I couldn't hold my breath any longer, and Chase was in trouble, choking on smoke. My eyes burned as tears dissipated in the heat. I blinked, noticing a lighter spot ahead. I aimed for it, coming out of the fiery curtain just in time to hit a ditch that brought us to an abrupt halt and tipped the Hummer on its side not two feet from a large tree.

The fire shifted away from us as I grabbed Chase, now pressed up against the passenger door, gasping for air. He got his feet under him, and we climbed out my side, moved away, and collapsed.

Too close!

Chase's hair looked singed. I coughed a few times and started beating him on the back to dislodge the smoke he'd inhaled. We sat there on the dirt path, holding each other and not saying a word until Gunn's deputy drove up and pulled the Hummer out of the ditch with his dualie. It had several major dents on the right side, but was drivable, even though in desperate need of alignment.

"That fire was deliberately set."

"No freakin' kidding," Chase gasped out between coughs. There was little doubt about who started it.

We drove back to the camper and noticed the door wide open. We pulled our guns and went in, finding the place trashed: the sheets slit, all the food poured out on the floor, and mirror glass shattered on the couch and bed.

"I guess he got out of the woods," Chase said.

"Or maybe, we've got more than one enemy."

Chase looked at me. I wondered just how deeply involved Acme was with Nita. We now knew he was still hung up on her, and that he was a psychopath.

Could Nita have coerced him into killing her mother? It still seemed the most likely possibility.

And where is Homer?

I tore out the door and around the camper, calling for the hound in a pitiful, but loud whine. To my relief, he came running from the riverbank beyond the Banoak house, unscathed. Once he got to me I realize he'd been pelted with eggs, I supposed to subdue him. I hosed him off with a bar of Zest.

In the bathroom, Chase found an inhaler some doctor in Asheville had prescribed for his "possible asthma", and he breathed much more easily. We cleaned up the food and broken glass as well as we could while Homer napped outside.

After a while, Rice called. "Ms. Quicki is leaving her house now. Stay on the phone with me." After several minutes, he said, "She's heading in your direction."

"She's probably picking up Acme. Stay with her, but not too close. Maybe she'll lead us right to him." We hung up.

Chase and I pulled the old pickup we'd borrowed from Navel Face into a driveway and sat, waiting for her to pass. Forty-three minutes later, I pulled out behind her as Rice blinked his lights in my rearview.

"Let's back off a little. She seems to be going in a circle. Maybe she's spotted us, or is, at least, suspicious." We gave her more room without losing her. When we were in the country with no streetlights, I got closer, figuring she wouldn't recognize us in the old truck.

I saw her taillights flash and turn on to the familiar country roads I'd been driving during the investigation. She swung into the yard at her mother's house and sat there. She didn't get out. Nobody came and got in with her. We parked down the dark highway with our lights off for about twenty minutes.

"Okay, I'm going to ask her what she's doing. Why don't you

get in with Lamar so she'll think I'm alone?"

"Are you sure, Logan? She could have a gun in her lap," Chase warned.

"I doubt it. She'd get someone else to do her dirty work for her."

"Like Acme, for instance?"

"My thoughts exactly."

My tap on the window made Nita jump. "What the hell?"

"I didn't mean to scare you. I thought you saw me behind you."

"No. No, I didn't," she said, looking for my Hummer.

"Look, I know you're meeting Acme to warn him that we're after him."

"No. No, you've got it all wrong."

"Step out of the car, Nita."

"Why? I haven't done anything wrong. And this is *my* property!"

"I'm taking you in for questioning."

She sighed and got out, putting her hands on the car and spreading her legs. I began her Miranda rights, arresting her for obstruction of justice, which I hoped would stick, or at least make her talk.

Two shots rang out through the darkness, and I turned to watch Chase and Lamar head in the opposite direction, tires squealing. In the same second, Nita bolted before I could cuff her.

Damn it! I wanted to arrest her, but I wanted Acme more, and I assumed my sidekicks were in hot pursuit. I snatched Nita's keys so she couldn't drive her car and ran to the old truck, heading in the direction the men had gone. Trying to corral a suspect in the dark was getting old. My eyes played tricks on me. The damaged eye nerves jumped around like a frog leg in a hot frying pan.

Another frustrating night ultimately yielded nothing. Acme knew the territory and had hunted around these woods and the river all his life. Every shadow had me pointing my gun in its direction, never sure enough to shoot, but feeling like an easy target.

Gunn, who joined the fiasco, called in troopers and deputies from surrounding counties once again. We sat in vehicles along the roadways, hoping Acme would surface. I had the feeling he was somewhere getting a good night's sleep while we struggled to stay awake. We'd already played this game one time and lost. I was beyond pissed.

When the sun cracked and spilled over the countryside, we decided to take a break and let local reinforcements take a shift. We instructed them to call us if anything turned up. Lamar Rice had been ordered back to Raleigh, so we could no longer count on his help. Both frazzled, Chase and I fell across the bare camper mattress, too tired to get under the covers.

I woke up when my eye started throbbing from the sunshine making a direct hit on it. My legs were spread, and Chase's head lay in the crotch of my trousers. Any other time I wouldn't have minded, but there was no time for sex, or even thoughts of anything relaxing and pleasant. I nudged him, and we each dragged ourselves off the bed. I made high-test coffee and called in.

"Sheriff, any luck?"

"Hell no." He yawned. "There's too many places to hide out. And Nita never showed back up either. Somebody must have picked her up."

"I've got her car keys, so she won't be driving away. She's probably with Acme."

"The troopers are leaving to report to their day-time assignments. A few county deputies are staying put until you say otherwise. I've got to get some shuteye. I'll catch you later."

"Thanks. Chase and I are headed back in a few minutes. We lost Agent Rice, and the SBI can't send anyone else. The flu epidemic going through the force is sending some of them to the hospital, and the rest are involved in their own caseloads."

I heard a noise and peeked out to see Magnolia Rich polishing her black patent-leather shoes with a cold biscuit. An enticing bundle sat beside her on the camper step.

"Magnolia!"

She jumped.

"You near 'bout scared the livin' day lights outta me, Miss. I tries to be quiet."

"I was already up. You shouldn't have brought more food."

"It's fresh sourdough bread, still warm, and some hoop cheese too. I makes loaves ever weekend for some ladies to have for Sundy dinner. I makes an extry one for you, Miss. You enjoy it now." She smiled and started to walk away, limping as she called to a cute little boy, probably a grandson, or maybe a great-grandson, throwing rocks. "Leroy! Come here! I told you not to get dirty. You gettin' a whoopin' when we gets home." A black puppy ran behind them. She turned back to me. "You haven't seen a puppy like this'n, have you? We missin' one."

"No, I haven't, but I'll let you know if one shows up. Thank you again, Miss Magnolia," I called after them.

I closed the door, turning to see Chase behind me with a grin and a large knife. We were both starved. Chase poured two mugs of coffee and fed Homer outside while I showered. The shower performed its magic, bringing my wilted body back to life. We ate hurriedly, even though I would have enjoyed taking my time with that warm bread and sharp cheese.

Chase jumped in the shower while I loaded ammo and checked radios. We grabbed the rest of the bread and cheese and split it into two packets to take with us, in case it turned into yet another long day. Chase headed off in one direction and I in another. I wanted to take another slow walk around the Banoak yard, feeling like I was missing something, but not knowing what it might be.

How many times have I felt this way?

Too many, I thought, kicking dirt. As I rounded the corner of the house, I saw Ethan, Lilith, and three other teens. The same ones I'd seen at the river.

"What's going on here?" They all threw down their shovels and looked at me as though I were the one out of place.

"We're digging up the yard, Agent Hunter," Ethan said.

"Yeah, lady. Why do you keep bothering us?" The boy dressed in black headed in my direction as if on a mission. He walked toward me and stopped a few feet away. "Leave us alone! Don't you have anything better to do?"

What are these kids doing that would upset him so much?

"Shut up, Austin!" Ethan glared at his friend until he backed away, muttering a few profanities in the process. Ethan approached me. "Look, Agent Hunter, Nita... I mean, Ms. Quicki, hired us to hunt for money she thinks is buried out here some place. She bought us the shovels. Go ask her."

"She told me she was going to dig, but I didn't know she planned on hiring help."

"Yeah, she did," Ethan said, seeming a little calmer. The others nodded silently. "This here's Austin Critcher." He pointed to the boy who'd spoken out. He just stared at me with that same hostile face, but I saw that his black pants had a tear in them.

Would that match the fabric I picked up at the pet graves?

"Over there is Huey LeFever. They're friends of mine. Nita asked me to find a few extra folks to get the job done." He motioned toward the blonde. "That's Olive Henry, and you already know Lilith."

"Nice to meet you all officially." I looked into the young faces, not as pale as before, and all wearing non-Goth clothes this time, except for Austin.

Ethan didn't mention the scene at the river, and I didn't either. However, I intended to find out more about this bizarre group, Austin Critcher in particular.

"Where's the other agent?"

"You mean Agent Railey? He's taking care of some business. He should be back any minute." He nodded. "Well, I'll get out of your way. Good luck."

I left, but something just didn't feel right; my insides still niggled.

Why all the anger from Austin? And does Hawk Daw have any idea where Ethan is and how odd his friends are?

The cold breeze hit me from every angle, feeling refreshing, and yet stinging me with the awareness that Christmas was only two weeks away, and Clara Banoak's murder hadn't been solved; nor had Cy's. I didn't want either case to go cold. I drank the last can of lite beer, hoping Chase and Homer picked up more while in Burgaw, hunting for fresh meat and spuds to grill. We'd all lost enough weight. It was hard to maintain balance with killers on the loose. It would be nice to replenish all the food and supplies we lost during the break-in.

I'd missed too many meals, and I could even tell I was getting dehydrated. Even though I tried to keep water nearby, I was often on the run with nothing but one of Chase's grain cakes and one bottle of water—and that's when I got lucky. We needed to replenish survival food in both vehicles too. If I got weak, I got careless and not alert to things I would usually observe easily.

I dragged myself up as Chase pulled into the yard and parked beside the camper.

"Meat! Real meat!" he called through his Jeep window, grinning like a hunter who'd just bagged a trophy, except that his meat was wrapped in cellophane with a price sticker. Homer barked with a delighted tail wagging him from side to side. "These are big and beautiful. And fresh."

I took the three steaks while he grabbed the other bags and charcoal. I smiled as he handed me a six-pack of beer to cool. I gave him a kiss. He grabbed two cases of water, one for his Jeep and one for the Hummer. I ratted through the paper bag. To my delight, he'd bought granola bars. How I did love this man! I planted a big kiss on his scrumptious lips.

"Well, if I'd known groceries turned you on, I'd have gone

to the store sooner." I smirked. "Now if Homer plants one of his slobbery kisses on me, I'm going to be sick."

I giggled.

"You got three steaks. Don't you think you're spoiling that hound a little too much?"

"Homer deserves a steak, don't you, boy?"

Homer agreed and slobbered on Chase's arm. "Give me a minute to cook it for you, big guy."

"Don't make a habit of it. We won't be able to afford him if he gets used to steak."

"Don't worry. I bought a new bag of dog food since the other one was ripped apart. This is a once-in-a-while treat. He's been through a lot too, you know."

I couldn't disagree with that. I watched as Homer toured the yard, peeing every few steps. I was always amazed at how much he could store up.

The meal was glorious and the dessert even better—not only sweet but passionate. I fell asleep not caring about anything but the man curled up next to me.

When I opened the camper door the following morning, I nearly stepped on a small package wrapped in plastic. I looked around the yard.

Nobody.

I lifted the package gingerly, making sure it wasn't some kind of booby trap. I pulled the plastic away. A post-it-note was attached to four homemade applejacks:

I hopes you enjoy these.

You needs some meat on your bones.

M

Magnolia Rich must have slipped in and out of the yard with the stealth of a cat. I could hardly wait to brew coffee and chow down. She was spoiling us, and it made the current situation a little more bearable.

Twenty-Two

Gunn called and said Acme was heading toward his property. Chase and I picked up the tail and followed him back to his house, being careful not to let him spot us. He had to know we would catch up with him eventually. I'd have thought he had better sense than to return to his own house. Something had to be drawing him back. He seemed to be on a mission. We parked out of sight behind some trees. Gunn walked up beside us, having parked elsewhere.

Acme had gone into the barn by the time we reached the yard, where several unoccupied vehicles were parked. We crept toward the commotion coming from the barn. Chase and Gunn eased around opposite sides of the barn while I approached the front with my gun drawn.

I peeked in. I wasn't sure what I was observing. Nita, gagged and tied up, squirmed in an old rotting cane chair while Acme and Hawk Daw quarreled. While they were distracted, I eased behind some big hay bales just inside the barn.

Nita struggled and tried to talk through the duct tape, to no avail, but I heard the quarrel loud and clear.

"Get off me, Acme! She...this bitch has been having sex with Ethan. Ethan!" Hawk yelled in Nita's face. "He's fifteen, for Christ's sake!"

He slapped her face, evidently not for the first time based on the red marks. Acme looked at Nita, obviously thunderstruck, as his eyes filled with tears. Then he unexpectedly turned and forklifted Hawk with his strong arms, ramming him into the barn wall some distance away. Hawk head-butted Acme, sending him to the ground in a daze. He walked back to Nita and slapped her again. Tears poured down her blistered face but the tape remained secure.

"Stop it, Dad!"

I recognized Ethan's voice, but he hadn't stepped inside the barn yet. I crouched down as he passed me, and made eye contact with Nita for the first time, easily seeing the fear in hers.

Acme stirred, but didn't get on his feet. Ethan marched to his father.

"Let Nita go."

"Hell no! Ethan, don't you get it, son? Nita's a child molester. You can't seriously want to help her."

Ethan continued to walk toward Nita. "What are you planning to do to her? Kill her? You've hurt her enough." He was about to pull the tape off her mouth when Hawk pushed him hard, knocking him into the side of the barn. Ethan stayed put as Acme got to his feet and rushed Hawk, knocking him off-balance.

They rolled around, collecting hay and other debris as they went. I was about to step out with my gun when I realized Ethan was peculiarly still, and blood poured from somewhere, already soaking the ground behind him.

"Ethan!" I glanced at Hawk and Acme, and ran to the boy, moaning pitifully. Hawk cold-cocked Acme and joined me.

Chase and the sheriff ran into the barn and snatched Acme up and cuffed him.

"Acme Beavers, you're under arrest for murder, assault, arson, and kidnapping. You have the right to remain silent."

Gunn continued the Miranda rights as he escorted Acme to the cruiser. Chase joined Hawk and I as we realized Ethan was impaled on the tines of a pitchfork. Hawk, his hands to his head, sobbed and mumbled apologies to Ethan.

"I'll call for a unit," I said.

"No! That'll take too long. My truck. I'll take him in the

truck," Hawk whimpered through sobs.

Chase and I helped ease Ethan into the truck he had driven up near the barn door, deciding to leave the tines in place until they reached the emergency room at least twenty miles away.

As Hawk drove off, a loud blast startled us, and I reached instinctively for my gun. Dick Leak stood in the barn's doorway with a shotgun. I watched in horror as Nita Quicki fell over in her chair from a perfect shot to the head.

"A brazen hussy! She needed to die for messing with that boy!" Dick Leak had the look of a madman.

I aimed my gun, anticipating he'd turn his on me next. But, instead, he lowered his arm to his side.

"Why, Mr. Leak?"

"She wouldn't pay up. I told her not to try to outsmart me. No, siree. I seen them two. I knowed all about it." Leak's voice frightened me, not to mention that he seemed to be hearing me just fine now. He wasn't deaf at all.

Chase eased over in the doorway behind the man, ready to take him down, but I signaled him to stay back until Leak spilled his guts.

"She wouldn't never go out with me, or even have supper with me. I just wanted to be friends, you know? She slept with ever man in these parts but me and Blood.

"Nice body too, and she knowed it. I've been watching her for years. She always took care of herself. She'd stand in front of the mirror naked and take pride in what she saw, back when she lived here. She kept the curtains open all the time just to tease me. She knowed I was watching. Had to. She's always been sexy since she was a little girl. Too much of that sex hormone, you know? She'd have sex with anybody but me."

His voice got louder and his body twitched.

"Even that kid. She's nothing but trash! Miss, you're smart. In time you would have figured it out. Nita made that boy's wildest dreams come true just so's she could use him. She sweet-talked that boy into doing the dirty work. Those friends of his were in on it too. She thought she was gone have a bankful of money. Ha!"

His voice quivered. "I'm just tired now. Tired of them, and tired of the whole infernal mess. I want it to be over with. I came here to end it all."

"Mr. Leak, put the gun down," I said, taking a step toward him.

"No! And you ain't locking me up for killing Cyrano neither. He deserved it."

"You killed Cy?" My blood boiled. "Why did you do that, you miserable...?" I stopped, finding it difficult to control my anger.

"He kept complaining about my Rhode Island Reds getting into his yard and crapping all over the place. He accused them of eating up his garden, but I know full well them infernal rabbits did it. Why, he told me he cooked and et one of my prize chickens."

"You killed a man for eating a chicken?"

"Not just *any* chicken, my prize chicken! That chicken won a prize at the fair every damn year. She weren't meant to be et."

My gun shook with fury as I faltered and Chase took a step closer behind Leak.

"Cyrano knew it would rile me. Me and him has had a feud going for years. I knew he was a drunk so's I laced his Wild Turkey with antifreeze and left it where he could grab it after we argued." He straightened up and stared at me. His eyes bulged. "I didn't figure I had enough conscience to be bothered with it, but I was wrong. Killing Cyrano was wrong."

He put the barrel of the shotgun in his mouth as I rushed at him, Chase running behind him. *Click. Click.* The gun jammed as Chase cut Leak's legs out from under him. I cuffed him, feeling like slapping the man senseless, but instead shoved him toward Chase, and went to check Nita's pulse, already knowing I wouldn't find one.

Once the rest of Gunn's crew arrived and cordoned off the latest crime scene, Chase and I rode to the hospital in silence, both exhausted and dumbfounded. But we knew we had to do this, and then collect the evidence needed for a conviction.

When we found Hawk at the hospital, he was the palest man I'd ever seen. He rushed over when he saw me. "I hurt Ethan. Bad." He buried his face in my shoulder and wept.

"You didn't mean to. It was an accident."

"I was so steamed. I couldn't believe Nita seduced him. She had plenty of grown men to choose from, for Christ's sake!"

"We need to talk," I said, touching his shoulder. "Let's go over to that bench."

He nodded and followed us outside, not knowing yet what the conversation would entail. Chase backed away, but stayed close enough to make certain Hawk didn't over-react to my next words.

"Hawk, we think we know who killed Clara Banoak."

"Nita paid Leak to do it, didn't she? That sorry piece of shit scumbag!"

"No, Hawk. According to Leak, Nita seduced Ethan, and talked him into killing Cla…"

"No! You don't believe that! You don't believe that son of a bitch Leak, do you?"

"Hawk, he tried to blow his brains out after he told me. Chase heard everything."

Hawk looked up at Chase, who nodded.

"Leak was blackmailing Nita because he'd seen her with Ethan, and maybe even saw Ethan at Clara's that night. He said he'd seen them together, and Nita manipulated Ethan into killing her mother. We think his friends may be involved too."

"It's a lie! Ethan wouldn't do something like that."

"Well, he did tell me how much he hated Clara, especially after the letter she wrote him. And, Hawk, I've seen some of Ethan's activities with his Goth friends. Remember when I told you I was concerned about him?"

"Why are you picking on Ethan? Kicking him when he's hurt?"

"Hawk, she used him. Offer a fifteen-year-old boy sex and he'll do just about anything."

Enough said for the moment.

Ethan had been pierced in the back by several tines, miraculously missing vital organs and the spine. We stayed in the waiting room as Hawk dialed family and friends and asked them not to come to the hospital.

When a nurse appeared to tell Hawk he could go in, I tugged his arm.

"I need to ask him some questions."

He hesitated, sighed, and finally nodded.

"Without you present."

He glared at me.

"Stay here with Chase, Hawk."

"But..."

"It's necessary, man. Logan won't take long," Chase told him.

Hawk walked off, holding his head down.

I entered the room and walked over to Ethan, propped on his side with several pillows. The bloody bandages looked bad, but the nurse assured me he would be fine.

"Ethan, we need to talk."

His eyes met mine.

"Yeah."

"Tell me what happened. I want to know about your relationship with Nita, torturing animals..."

"You know about all that?" He tried to turn, but winced in pain instead.

"Yes. I saw you and Nita kissing down by the river. I saw shallow animal graves and torn black fabric like you and your friends wore when I saw you sniggling for catfish, or whatever that really was you all were doing."

"Agent Hunter, I don't know what made me do it. Nita had

been talking to me a little bit about how nice it would be to be rich when her mother died. She was always trying to talk me into doing something to Mrs. Banoak, but she didn't want to know the details, you know? So she wouldn't be implicated."

"So Nita talked you into offing her mother."

"Well, not exactly." Ethan grimaced and turned on his back.

I gently pulled the pillows up behind him before making eye contact again. Chase and Hawk stepped into the room and closed the door about the time I remembered I was questioning a minor, not an adult.

"Ethan, do you want an attorney present?" I glanced at Hawk.

"No," Ethan said, only giving his father a quick glance. "I want to get this out of my system. I know I need some help."

Hawk walked over to his son and held his hand. "It's okay, son. The nightmare's over." Hawk looked at me sternly. "Why would you think he needs a lawyer?"

"Dad, please let me talk to these agents alone. What you need to know is I did some bad things. Very bad. I have to answer for them."

"What are you talking about? Has Agent Hunter filled your head with guilt?"

"No, I already had plenty of that. But, Dad, I can't get through this with you standing there looking at me. Please go outside. And, Dad, I love you. I'm sorry I shamed you."

"Shamed me? Son, you're the most important thing in my life. What the hell are you talking about?" Chase pulled on Hawk's arm but he snatched away. "Okay. Son, don't say another word to these agents. I'm getting you a lawyer."

He pulled out his cell phone and dialed. The rest of us stayed quiet until attorney-at-law, Houston Warren arrived, smelling like a rotten cigar. After Ethan and Hawk conferred with Mr. Warren, the questioning continued with the attorney present.

"Okay, Ethan, let's get back to Nita trying to get you to kill

Clara Banoak." He saw the PDA I would use to record him. "You said she didn't 'exactly' talk you in to it. What did you mean by that?"

"Nita had been wanting her mother to die somehow, but what really made me do it was when Mrs. Banoak threatened me."

"Clara Banoak threatened you? When and why?"

"It was after a ritual. You know, Agent Hunter, you walked up on us when we were drowning a puppy."

"What?"

I jerked backwards as Hawk's voice boomed from the windowsill and he jumped into his son's face.

"Dad, please leave!" Ethan was in noticeable pain, but he and Hawk held each other's moist eyes for a long moment before Ethan cut his eyes at me.

"Please make him leave. I can't do this with him in here!"

After Hawk and Mr. Warren whispered, Hawk reluctantly left the room with a heart-broken demeanor and plenty of fear in his eyes. Chase followed him out, nodding at me.

"Now, Ethan. Let's see if we can get through this without any more interruptions, and then you can get some rest. I thought you guys were sniggling for catfish. That was a puppy?"

"Yeah. It belonged to Leroy Rich."

"Magnolia Rich's grandson?"

"Yeah. We stole several small animals and tortured them as part of a stupid ritual. I was elected alpha male of the group. A bunch of stupid crap all led to this." His tears burst out and streaked his young face. "When you came up, Austin was drowning the puppy, but since we figured you thought it was a catfish, we played along. Austin turned it loose under a branch and it floated away. That's when he told you the catfish got away."

I blinked in disbelief and Mr. Warren's mouth fell open.

"Old lady Banoak hid in the woods that night and confronted us. She said she was gone call our parents and Sheriff Gunn the next morning. Lilith didn't care, but Austin and Olive said their parents would kill them. We decided to take care of her before she had the chance to call anybody."

"What night was that, Ethan?"

"The night we killed her," he said it in a whisper, but Mr. Warren and I both reacted as if he shouted the admission. I felt the color seep from my face.

Ethan continued after a sip of water. "Olive was falling apart, so we took her home but swore her to secrecy. Huey said his dad had a gambrel, but he hadn't used it all year. We put on thick work gloves, went and got the gambrel out of his daddy's barn, and made a plan. I snuck back into my bedroom and got the deer gutting stuff while Dad was watching a ballgame."

"What time of night was this?"

"About 11:30."

"You don't have a curfew?"

"Nah. I can stay out as late as I want, especially on the weekends. Anyways, Huey, Austin, Lilith, and me knew we needed to make it look like somebody else did it, so we knocked on the door, and Lilith threw the spotlight on to blind Mrs. Banoak while Austin and I overpowered her. I knocked her to the floor and hit her on the head, so she would be knocked out for the rest of it. Huey stabbed her just to make sure she didn't come to and start screaming or something.

"We slit her just like we would a deer. We took her up and put her over the balcony. I figured it would be more, I don't know, dramatic, I guess. Austin rigged up the hook and we just let her drop. Her innards spattered all over the floor." Ethan's head dropped. "I can't believe we did it. We got caught up somehow."

He took a sip of water. "Huey and I panicked when we saw all that blood. We ran down the stairs and out the door with Austin and Lilith. We forgot about the spotlight in the bushes." He sighed. "I've had nightmares ever since."

"Did Nita know you killed her mother?"

"Yeah. But she didn't act like she was too happy about it when all was said and done. It was like she wanted her dead, but, then again, she didn't, you know?" Again, his face dropped, and he cupped it in his hands and let the sobs flow.

Houston Warren stepped in my face. "Shit fire, Agent Hunter, the boy's only fifteen! The whole dang crowd is underage."

"I know, but this is a heinous crime, Mr. Warren. Ethan's co-operated with us, so maybe that will help his case."

I looked back at Ethan. "Thank you for telling the truth."

"Agent Hunter, I don't want the rest of them to be in trouble. I'm taking all the blame," Ethan announced with conviction.

"I'm sorry, son, but it doesn't work that way."

I left the room and Hawk flew past me to confer with Ethan and his son's attorney. Chase and I called Sheriff Gunn to pick up the other teenagers and get search warrants for their homes. They would have to answer for the animal torture as well. This time I could understand Clara Banoak's fury.

Twenty-Three

In addition to assaulting and kidnapping a law-enforcement officer, Acme Beavers would face charges of some kind for the remains in the barn, even though we now knew he hadn't killed his parents or Clara Banoak. He would be charged for arson as well.

Dick Leak, who admitted to the deafness pretense, was pushing seventy-five-years-old, and would stand trial for the murder of Nita Quicki. He had already admitted to poisoning Cyrano because of an on-going argument over the property lines, chickens, and Cy's agitation with Leak's constant snooping. The small county jail posted a suicide watch.

Ethan Daw was placed in juvenile detention without bail. A court would decide whether or not to try him as an adult because of the viciousness of Clara Banoak's murder. He could end up on death row, but I felt sure the fact that a forty-five-year-old woman seduced him and planted the seeds of murder would help lessen his sentence. I wasn't sure yet how I felt about his future. I had some issues to work out.

His Goth friends, Austin, Huey, and Lilith, were charged with "acting in concert with" Ethan. That meant they would all be charged with murder. Too bad they let peer pressure and a desire for acceptance ruin their young lives too. Olive Henry got off easier since she hadn't been with them at the time of the murder, but she had some liability since she knew about it and did nothing to stop it.

In the wee hours of the morning, Chase and I settled into the same bed in our miniature camper, holding each other and saying little while Homer snoozed, his chin resting on my thigh. The investigation ended, but neither of us could feel anything more than relief coupled with sadness.

The radio weather alert warned of downbursts and possible tornados due to frontal systems on a collision course. That didn't help us relax. After a strong gust that rocked the camper, the wind calmed enough to rock us to sleep.

When Chase rustled me awake, I tried to focus on something bright, making my eye hurt. A silver box opened in front of my face. I looked at its contents and at a grinning Chase.

"I know I proposed to you and you accepted, but I never got around to picking out the ring. I took this out from under the tree because I couldn't wait until Christmas to give it to you."

I lifted the large solitaire from the box and turned it in every direction.

"Chase! You shouldn't have done this. This must have cost a fortune! I told you a band was fine with me."

"This is Mother's. She wants you to have it. She hopes it will bring you more happiness than it ever did her." His eyes filled with tears. "I told her I'd make sure you were happy every day of my life."

I fell into his arms and we both cried. I called my mother to tell her I was finally getting married and she would need a new dress. She seemed delighted and asked me to put Chase on the phone so she could give him an official interrogation. I refused but promised to bring Chase to see her soon.

After a while we walked through the Banoak yard, hand in hand, one last time. We stepped around a few mud puddles and noticed the taller trees in the yard had lost quite a few limbs during the unusual winter storm, but there didn't appear to be any damage to the house.

We turned as Hawk Daw pulled up the drive in his truck, stepped out, and hung his head.

"I heard you were getting ready to pull out. Agent Hunter, you were right. Ethan was in that Goth mess. You tried to tell me. I didn't want to believe it. He killed cats and dogs. That's bad enough, but to kill another human being, well…" He yanked at his hair, his face distorted.

After pacing around a few times, he came to a stop in front of Chase, a man deflated like a ruptured balloon. "It's all my fault. I caused every bit of this."

"No, man," Chase said.

"How could that be, Hawk?" I wanted to hear what he had come to say.

"I encouraged Ethan to hate her," he said softly. "I didn't supervise him close enough either. Hell, I guess I must not have supervised him at all, from all he's telling. I figured we're out here in the country, you know, and he can't get into anything that would hurt him. I never guessed he'd be the one doing the hurting. I trusted him, Logan." His face fell into his callused hands and his broken heart poured into them.

Chase tried to console Hawk while I walked off. Yes, parents do bear the responsibility of where their teenagers are after midnight. I'd seen it too many times. Letting them break laws like driving without a license often leads to breaking other laws. The kids figure their parents will get them out of any trouble they get into. Well, not this time. Ethan and his cohorts would probably be tried as adults in the murder of Clara Banoak.

The men talked quietly for a few minutes and then Hawk waved and left. Chase joined me and we went to look for Homer. We found him relieving himself on every tree and zipping around after some paper in the air.

Green paper. *Familiar green paper.*

Chase snatched at it as money zipped by. Lots of green cash.

We dashed around to the side of the house where the constant cash flow came from. The wind had apparently blown the loose *Boston Whales 1875* sign off the rickety shed sometime during the night. Bills of every denomination soared out of the space behind where it had been located, and up into trees and down the river.

Chase tried to catch as many as he could while I walked the path to the graves of Eli and Clara Banoak, covered now with a blanket of cold cash. The sight made me laugh, and Chase soon joined me while Homer began to bay with glee behind us. All the digging Nita and the kids insisted on doing had been unnecessary. Eli had hidden his cash in the shed, right over Nita's nose.

We collected as many bills as possible and called Sheriff Gunn to pick up the money. He counted over twenty thousand dollars, but much more may have blown away during the high wind before we noticed it. Possibly hundreds of thousands.

At dusk, Chase hitched the camper and we towed it out of Ivanhoe with some degree of satisfaction that the killers, although juveniles, had been caught, that justice would be done, and that these Black River dwellers had the promise of better chapters in their lives.

It was time for us to have a few days of quiet time—if that were possible with Homer. I drew in a long breath of crisp country air, full of delightful thoughts of Christmas with the man I loved beside me.

About Author Susan Whitfield

Susan Whitfield is a life-long resident of North Carolina. She grew up in Pender County near Black River and now resides in Wayne County with her husband, Doyle. Whitfield published two other mystery novels, Genesis Beach and Just North of Luck, and is currently writing a fourth, set around Wilmington. Her Web site includes more information:

www.susanwhitfieldonline.com